Lord Danvers Investigates

A Tincture of Murder

DONNA FLETCHER CROW

Verity Press

A Tincture of Murder
Book 4, Lord Danvers Investigates

Copyright © 2012 by Donna Fletcher Crow

All rights reserved as permitted under the U.S. Copyright Act of 1976. No part of this publication may be reproduced or transmitted in any form or by any means, electronic or mechanical, including photocopy recording or any information storage and retrieval system, without permission in writing from the publisher. The only exception is brief quotations in printed reviews.

First Printing 2012
Greenbrier Book Company
New Bern, NC 28561

Second Printing 2017
Verity Press
an imprint of Publications Marketing, Inc.
Box 972
Boise, Idaho 83704

Cover design and layout by Ken Raney

This is a work of fiction. The characters and events portrayed in this book are fictitious or used fictitiously.

❀ Created with Vellum

WHAT READERS ARE SAYING
ABOUT LORD DANVERS
INVESTIGATES

"A compelling story peopled with interesting characters and vivid details drawn from impeccable research. Victorian Britain comes to life, thanks to period dialogue that rings all the right notes and a mystery that keeps you guessing until the very last page. Delightful!" - Liz Curtis Higgs, *New York Times* best-selling author of *Mine Is the Night*

"The historical setting is authentic and allows the reader a glimpse, without overwhelming. An enjoyable book which entertains and delights. - Wendy Jones, The DI Shona McKenzie Mysteries

"Donna Fletcher Crow's settings are impeccable, every detail accurate, so the reader can enjoy and be enthralled by the deliciously tangled tale she weaves... a spider-web of interlocking crimes and family secrets, all satisfactorily resolved at the end. A thoroughly delightful excursion by an accomplished storyteller." - Dorothy Stewart, *When The Boats Come Home*

"A fascinating journey into the daily lives of nineteenth-century British aristocrats and their servants... believable fictional characters and scenes embellish the true stories of real-life individuals. Detailed descriptions, seamlessly woven into the story, made the book believable as well as visual." - Becky

"A quick, entertaining read with believable characters." - Old movie fan

"Beautifully evocative and well-researched." - Sheila

"An entertaining read for all audiences. Highly recommended." - Janet

"The author's ability to put the reader into history is remarkable." - Amazon customer

"When you pick up a period mystery you want to experience all that period has to offer. Donna Fletcher Crow delivers on that expected promise, weaving details about clothing, decorative style, and odors—so many odors! Add taste and touch, and you have an idea of how thorough this author is when it comes to her ability to weave the threads of the mystery together. She writes with such attention to detail that you're constantly analyzing new evidence and never certain that you're on the right track. The surprise ending is truly that. I gave it five stars because of the intricacy of the storytelling, and the fact that this is a mystery that makes you think even after you've read the last word." - J L

To Ken Raney,
cover artist and formatter extraordinaire,
adviser and friend

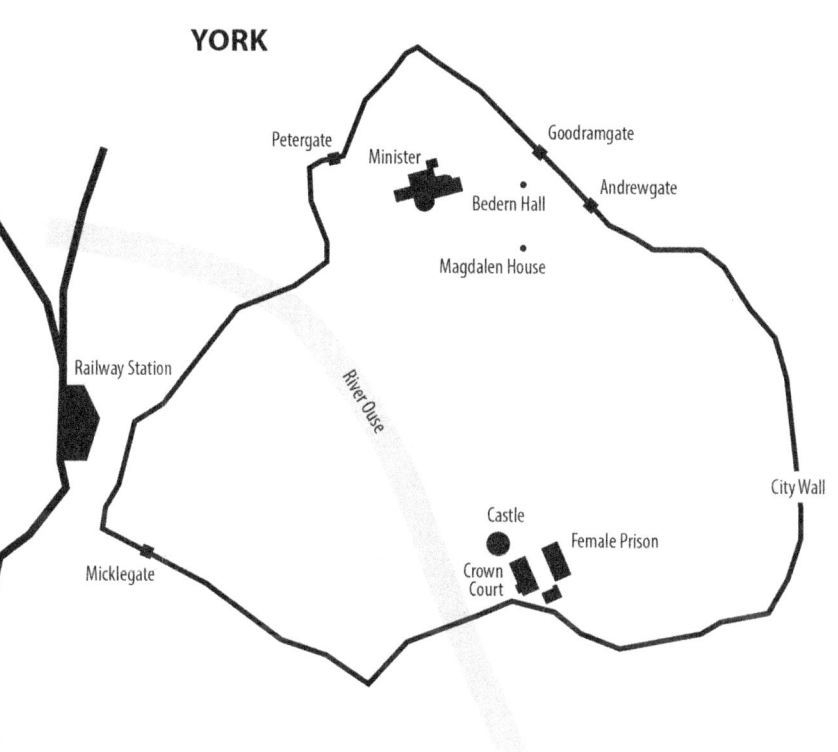

YORK

Wandseley Hall

Petergate

Minister

Goodramgate

Andrewgate

Bedern Hall

Magdalen House

Railway Station

River Ouse

City Wall

Castle

Female Prison

Crown Court

Micklegate

CHARACTERS

Lord Charles Leighton, 9th Viscount Danvers
Lady Antonia Danvers, his wife
The Honourable Charles Frederick (Charlie) Leighton, their infant son
Sara Bevans, his nurse
Hardy, Danvers's manservant
Isabella, Lady Danvers's maid
Aelfrida, the Dowager Duchess of Aethelbert
The Honourable Reverend Frederick William (Freddie) Leighton, Lord Danvers's brother
Bracken, butler at Norwood Park
Sir Gerald Wandseley
Lady Philomena Wandseley
Humber, Wandseley Hall butler
Polly Summers, Wandseley Hall maid
Baroness Carlotta Billingston, patroness of Magdalen House
Mr. Sylvester Billingston, her husband
Mrs. Selby, Wandseley Hall Housekeeper
Mrs. Foss, Wandseley Hall cook
Sergeant Carlton, York Police

Isa, Magdalen House night nurse
Betsy, Iris, Verd, Nan, Magdalen House clients
Victoria Hever, Freddie's friend
Cecilia Hever, her twin sister
Millie Carter, inhabitant of Bedern
Joey, Floss, Tim, Sukey, Lettie, her siblings
Mrs. Elton, Billingston's cook
Mr. George Pimm, Director of York Industrial Ragged School
Louisa, maid at Industrial school
Baron George William Wilshere Bramwell, Judge
William Dove, the accused
Mr. Overend, counsel for the prosecution
Mr. Bliss, defense counsel
Harriet Dove, victim
Mary Wood, Dove's nurse
Henry Harrison, witch doctor
Madge Broadbent, abortionist
*Historical characters listed in italics

"What a perfect evening." Antonia, Lady Danvers, gave a small, delicious sigh of pleasure and rested her head on her husband's broad shoulder as the landau, tonight open to the stars, rolled through the Northamptonshire countryside under the steady driving of Charles's ever-efficient man Hardy. "Oh, Charles, such a lovely ball." She closed her eyes and saw again the swirl of wide, crinoline gowns swaying like bells under the gleaming crystal chandeliers.

"Glad I talked you into attending, then, my love?"

Antonia more felt than saw her husband's smile from his face several inches above hers. She smoothed the primrose silk of her skirt, spread out to fill the carriage. "Of course I am. It was never that I didn't want to attend the ball, you understand, but simply that I'm so content." She smiled at her own words. That one who had formerly been so restless anywhere but in the whirl of London society could know such contentment living quietly at the Danvers family seat deep in the countryside month after month...

Charles's arm drew tighter around her. "Charlie." He said simply.

"Charlie." She agreed. And even as she said it her arms ached for the seven-month-old son whose birth they had so long desired. In spite of the excellent attentions of Nurse Bevans to the infant, Antonia disliked being away from her enchanting child for any extended period. Every smile and gurgle she missed would be lost forever.

Antonia's euphoric smile deepened as above her head her husband burst into a deep-throated, almost on-key rendition of *Soa Gân*, the traditional Welsh lullaby he had sung to a cooing Charles Frederick almost every night since his birth:

"*Sleep our baby, at the breast,*
'Tis mother's arms around you.
Harm will ne'er meet you in sleep,
Hurt will always pass you by.
Child beloved, always you'll keep,
Sleep in peace tonight, sleep."

Charles's happiness added to Tonia's gratification as did the fact that he had of recent months abandoned his passion to break forth in operatic aria for a quieter mode of expression. "My love," she began, then hesitated. She hated to break the tranquility by introducing a subject of discord. And yet, what better time? They were alone together, nothing to interrupt them... "My love, about the letter from Frederick..."

The singing broke off abruptly. "Dash that young puppy. What could have possessed him to take up residence in darkest Yorkshire?"

Tonia gave a trill of laughter to offset what she knew to be her husband's agitation. Only the strongest feeling would lead him to such overstatement. "Hardly that, I think. I've always found York to be one of the most charming cities in the kingdom."

"To visit, certainly. But why Freddie should be so pudding-headed as to choose to live so far away from all his family and friends. And after we did him the singular honour of naming our son and heir after him."

Antonia laughed again. "You do forget yourself, my love. Aside from the Charles part, I believe Frederick is one of your names as well. As it has been for every male in your line for how many generations?"

"That is entirely beside the point. If my brother has gotten himself into a scrape with some lightskirt in York it's up to him to disentangle himself. Be good experience for him. There is absolutely no reason I should dash halfway across the country for Freddie's pleasure and my own discomfort."

Tonia bit her tongue. Charles didn't need reminding that since his father, the 10th Earl, had effectively abdicated his title by choosing to live in Paris, his eldest son, the Viscount, was head of the family for all intents and purposes. As a matter of fact, she suspected that his discomforture at being thrust into that position was precisely what lay behind her husband's strong reaction to his younger brother's eccentric move.

She chose another line of attack. "Really, Charles. Frederick is a vicar. I can't imagine a more respectable position. The trouble on which he has sought your counsel can't possibly be of the nature you imply."

A firm "Humph" signaled that the conversation was at an end.

Antonia allowed her mind to drift back to happier thoughts as the carriage turned off the main road and began the ascent up the mile-long, elm-lined lane to Norwood Park, and Charles resumed his interrupted lullaby:

"*Sleep child mine, there's nothing here,*
While in slumber you are blest,
Angels smiling, have no fear,
Holy angels guard your rest."

3

Tonia was never certain what instinct caused her to sit upright and scan the night sky ahead of them. Did it somehow seem too light? Or the air to warm a bit? Perhaps there was the tiniest whiff of acrid scent on the breeze? Whatever the cause, suddenly every nerve in her body was electrified.

"Hardy, spur on the horses. Hurry!" She sat forward, straining to haste their progress.

A horrified cry broke from her as the carriage swung around the last curve of the drive.

A billow of smoke rose from the east wing of the house—the wing where the infant Charlie lay asleep in the nursery—and an unnatural, yellow light flickering behind the curtains confirmed that Norwood Park was on fire.

With a crack of Hardy's whip the horses jolted forward. Danvers jumped to his feet and was out of the carriage before the wheels had crunched to a stop on the gravel drive. *No! God, no!* His whole being cried out as he raced forward, oblivious to any thought but that of his infant son asleep in the nursery at the far end of the second floor.

At the foot of the wide, curving stairwell he turned and shouted to Hardy only a few steps behind him. "Raise the alarm! The servants..." Without finishing his sentence he turned to face the smoke pouring down the stairs from the first floor. Clasping his linen handkerchief to his nose, he dashed upward, taking the marble steps two at a time.

A shriek from above his head drew him with even greater speed to the wooden staircase leading to the second floor. Sickening yellow light danced on the walls. "Help!" Sara Bevan's scream was accompanied by a baby's cry.

The stairwell turned and Danver's heart sank. A wall of flame at the top separated him from Sara and her precious armful. Danvers checked his forward rush for the space of a heartbeat.

"Here!" He whirled at the sound of Antonia's voice behind him.

Racing up the stairs, she thrust a handful of wet cloths into his hands. Then Charlie wailed.

With no thought for his own danger, Danvers simply lunged.

The mad plunge landed him on the far side of the flames. Had Sara not begun batting frantically at his hair with one hand as she clasped Charlie in the other Charles would not have realized his hair was on fire.

Charles flung one of the dripping cloths to the nurse as he pulled the baby from her arms and wrapped another well-soaked towel around the howling infant.

Danvers heart sank as he turned to face the flames. Even in those few seconds the inferno had gained in fury. He turned back. Perhaps the servants' stairs...

The quickest glance told him there was no escape. The fire had apparently spread both directions from the sitting room on the north side of the hall and now encircled them. They could reach no window even if they had a ladder. Roaring, crackling sounds filled the air and made it hard to think. His eyes watered. Smoke made him cough. Sweat poured off his face from the intense heat.

"We'll all be burnt!" Sara gave an hysterical sob.

Danvers grabbed her shoulder and shook her roughly. "Put the towel over your head. Follow me closely. Hurry!"

Without waiting to see if she obeyed he hugged Charlie to his chest and all but flew through the flames.

Sara followed him screaming and would have plunged straight on to the landing had not Hardy been there to catch her. Danvers clasped the brass handrail, then realized it was searing hot.

Eyes streaming, throat burning, head woozy from the smoke, Danvers paused at the landing and looked back just as the wall fell in where Nurse Bevans had been standing with Charlie in her arms only moments before.

The rest of the night was a blaze of writhing images highlighted by red-orange flames against the black night sky. Danvers remembered delivering Charlie into Antonia's arms; he remembered Hardy organizing the hastily roused servants into a bucket brigade as the groom Coacher brought the pump from the carriage house and pumped water from the ornamental pond.

He remembered in jumbled snatches rushing back toward the house to make certain all the servants were out and being stopped by the butler Bracken in his dressing gown who reported all accounted for. Then in memory the sound of the pump spraying water and the roar of the flames blended with the sound of Tonia standing near him on the lawn speaking soothing phrases to their son, and Isabella, Tonia's tiny, efficient maid, calming the hysterical Sara Bevans.

Charles took the lead from the pump hose and directed all the water to dowsing the west wing of the house, as it was clear the east could not be saved, although the servants had done all they could to rescue the heirlooms from the drawing room. Silhouettes of piled chairs, tables, urns, lamps... the amassment of generations of his ancestors, sprawled across the lawn like a misshapen sculpture garden.

Danvers never knew what triggered the realization, but suddenly he knew what was missing from the jumble of sights and sounds. Antonia's beloved red-gold terrier Tinker should have been everywhere getting underfoot, yapping and making a thorough nuisance of himself. With a sinking heart Charles realized that the pet Tonia lavished so much favor on must still be shut in the room he had occupied with his own brood. The scamp had hardly left their side since March when Tinker had become the proud father of a litter of four puppies—three golden like himself, one black and curly like the doe-eyed mother.

Danvers thrust the hose to Coacher and headed across the lawn toward the solar. The flames hadn't reached there yet. It would be the work of minutes to break a window and pull them out. Smoke billowed over his head and sparks snapped against the black sky like shooting stars as he rounded the end of the house. Above the crackle of the flames he thought he could hear a sharp yapping on the other side of the French windows.

Poised to break through the glass, he was thrown backward, shards of glass hurtling toward him, as the floor above him exploded. The blast threw Charles to the ground and an explosion of swirling lights filled his head.

"Charles!" Antonia, observing Hardy and Isabella ministering to the burns of servants who had been in the front line of fighting the flames, suddenly realized that Charles was not among the nursing or the nursed.

Antonia thrust the sleeping Charlie into his nurse's arms and raced toward the house. "No, m'lady," Hardy grabbed her shoulder and spun her around. "You'll not be going in. It's not safe, the whole top floor'll be coming down any moment."

Oblivious to all but the fact that Charles must be trapped somewhere in the smoking, black hulk that had been his home, she shook off Hardy's restraining hand and rushed forward. "Charles! Charles!" Was that a moan she heard? Acrid smoke made her cough. No, not a moan. A bark. "Tinker?" A chorus of small puppy yips confirmed the identity.

"Around to the back. M'lady!" Hardy led the way.

Following Tinker's insistent barks, they stumbled over broken timbers and scattered stones, bits of glass crunching under their feet in the pale pre-dawn grey.

"Here, m'lady." Hardy knelt over a limp, silent form.

Antonia clamped both hands to her mouth, too terrified to ask the question.

"He's alive." Her relief at Hardy's words was almost sufficient to make her swoon.

"Looks like the blast knocked him out." Hardy was tugging at a heavy timber that held Danvers's right leg pinned to the ground. "And can you be pulling his shoulders when I lift the beam, m'lady?"

Tonia knelt and grasped the broad shoulders. "On three, m'lady. One, two—" Antonia closed her eyes and tugged with all her strength. She could not have shifted the inert body more than a few inches before her hands slipped and she fell on to the wet, debris-littered grass. But Hardy's shout of triumph and Danvers's moan of returning consciousness were sweeter to her than any choral symphony.

Hours later they sat in a the smoky, but unburnt, west drawing room of Norwood Park with the doctor, hastily fetched by the footman. He made a face at the reek of smoke and singed hair still clinging to Danvers. "A good thing Nurse Bevans was as quick as you say to beat you about the head or you would have lost more of your beauty."

Whether Danvers's grimace was for the doctor's mild humor or the pain as he set to wrapping Danvers's elevated leg was unclear.

A short time later the doctor sat back with a satisfied nod. "There now, my lord. You're fortunate nothing is broken. But the bruise is deep—that falling beam probably bruised the bone. It will be painful for some time. Keep off it as much as you can for a few days and use a stick when you move about. Fortunate that your left hand got the worst of the burns. You can use your right hand for the stick."

Before Danvers could tell him what he thought of such a

plan, the doctor turned to Antonia and drew several packets of reddish-brown powders from his satchel. "Keep these, my lady. If the viscount has trouble sleeping, you may mix one sachet in a glass of alcohol and flavor it with cinnamon."

Bracken had barely escorted the doctor from the room before Danvers turned to Tonia with a scowl. "Don't bother, Tonia. I'll not take any of his nasty laudanum tincture. I'd as soon visit an opium den."

"Whatever you say, my love." Antonia gave her lord her sweetest smile and slipped the packets into her pocket. Having abandoned her ruined ball gown, Antonia wore the plainest of her day dresses, which Isabella had brought up from the laundry since little smoke had penetrated the basement.

Nurse Bevans had contrived something of a workable nursery in the red room, the room least contaminated with smoke, and Hardy had managed to calm Mrs. Bayard, the cook, and a kitchen maid sufficiently that Bracken could serve a light breakfast of tea, toast, coddled eggs and kippers. But really, the situation was impossible.

Antonia soon realized just how impossible it was a few hours later when Rowler, Danvers's estate agent, delivered a fuller report on the damage. "It's impossible to say what caused it, my lord. Perhaps someone being careless enough to leave a candle burning."

"Oh," Antonia's gasp was no more than a sharp intake of breath, but the constriction in her throat almost choked her. Could it have been her fault? She often used the small with-drawing room just down the hall from the nursery for her own study. Could she have left a candle near an open window? Did a guest of wind blow a drapery into the flame? She had had only a small fire on the grate to abate the chill of the late June evening, but perhaps...

She forced her mind back to Rowler's report, "You'll be

pleased to know that the central Tudor portion survived, my lord. It's in need of a thorough clearing of smoke and ash and repair of the water damage, as is the west wing. I fear the east requires a complete rebuilding."

Danvers shook his head. "That being the wing where we live. How long will it take to get the place habitable, man?" He struck the arm of his chair in a gesture of impatience.

"We'll need to make a more complete inventory, my lord, but we can hope for the best by Christmas, I should think."

"Christmas! And where are we to live in the meantime?" Danvers's craggy features looked sharper than ever under his scowl. "This is no time to remove to the London house with the summer heat coming on."

His look softened as he turned to Antonia. "It appears we must take a house. Where would you fancy living, my love?"

Antonia blanched. The thought of setting up house in hired premises held no charms for her. And Bracken and Rowler and much of the staff would be needed here for the rebuilding. "Surely it would be simplest to accept an invitation to a house-party." Tonia struggled to recall the invitations lining the now-demolished mantle in the upstairs withdrawing room. "I believe there was an invitation from Lady Saxe, and I remember that Baron Weaver sent a note..." Of course, the full house-party season wouldn't really start until the shooting in August.

Danvers groaned. "Fine guest I'd be—hobbling about on a stick."

"Well, there's family. Agatha..."

Charles groaned even louder and shifted impatiently in his chair. "Anyone but my sister."

"Perhaps it would do you good to take the waters at Harrogate, my love."

He made a face. "I have an injury; not an illness. Vile, chalybeate water." He shuddered.

"As were the waters at Tunbridge Wells, most assuredly. But we do have our darling Charlie as a result of my drinking those waters."

Danvers sighed. "And Harrogate just happens to be a few miles from York. You're back to my plaguing brother again, aren't you?"

"Another letter arrived in this morning's post, my love."

"Frederick again?"

"No, this one from Aunt Aelfrida. I fear that the stars may be in alignment against you. She, too, asks—well, demands, really—that you go to York."

Charles ran his fingers through his unruly black locks. "Don't tell me she wants to 'restore' York Minster?"

"I think that this time you will find yourself quite on the side of the Dowager Duchess of Aethelbert. She wants you to talk sense into Freddie. She insists his place is in a parish in London where he can assist Agatha in finding eligible males to marry your younger sisters."

Her husband's silence gave Antonia courage to press on. "Yorkshire is quite lovely this time of year." She allowed a small smile to play around her mouth.

"Very well, York it is." And then he brightened. "It would make a fine flight in the aerostat."

"Charles! You'll go by train like a proper invalid."

But it was clear he had hardly heard her. "A nice smooth aerostat ride will be much easier on my bruised bones than hobbling on and off pestilential trains, being covered in soot and shaken about. Hardy!"

Hardy entered with an alacrity that showed he hadn't been out of earshot. "And you can be certain I'll attempt the smoothest of landings, m'lord."

"I fear I shall have to see to my own landing, Hardy."

"But your hand, m'lord—"

Antonia cut him off with a sharp shake of her head.

"I am quite capable, man. You will be needed to accompany Isabella and Sara with the Honourable Charles Frederick on the train." How long had it been since he and Antonia had been alone together for any extended period of time? There could be more advantages to this plan than he had foreseen.

Hardy's face fell, the stiffness of his reply showing his disappointment. "Yes, m'lord."

"Hardy, you may send my brother a telegram to inform him of our arrival tomorrow. The impudent youth has taken the liberty to suggest we should accept the invitation of a Sir Gerald and Lady Wandseley, apparently his most supportive parishioners. We'll undoubtedly find ourselves in some crumbling ruin on a moor with the wind howling around it."

"I believe the term is *wuthering*, my love." Antonia attempted a small smile.

Danvers scowled at his wife as if she had taken leave of her senses. But she bent and kissed his wrinkled brow. "Don't take on so, I know you read Miss Brontë's novel after I returned it to the library shelves."

Danvers chose to ignore her. "I trust this Lord Wandseley's gardens will accommodate an aerostat landing. You may look him up in Debrett's and chart our course, Hardy."

4

Ah, it was so good to be out once again in his aerostat, the red and yellow striped canopy surrounded by the blue sky overhead and the smooth, green fields, broken by hedgerows and stone walls beneath. It was enough to make Danvers forget the devastation he left behind at Norwood Park. Almost enough to make him forget the throbbing in his right leg—until he moved without thought.

"Am I forgiven, my love?" Tonia smiled at him from her seat at the side of the gondola.

"Forgiven?" This was his Antonia. He could imagine nothing he wouldn't forgive.

"For siding with Frederick."

"Nothing to forgive you for—this was quite the best plan. But I won't be answerable for Frederick's safe conduct if he has besmirched the family name."

Tonia looked over the side of the wicker basket that held them suspended between earth and sky to observe the town below them. "Is that Nottingham?"

Danvers consulted his map, pocket watch and navigation

instruments. "Excellent! That is Doncaster and we are almost thirty minutes ahead of schedule."

Tonia's brow furrowed. "I trust we won't arrive ahead of Hardy. We shall need his flags to find our landing field." But even as she spoke, Antonia relaxed against the gondola walls. It was clear this excursion was precisely what they both needed.

A long trail of white smoke issuing from the tall smoke-stack of a tank engine pulling a string of passenger cars along the silver line of rail disappeared into the distance ahead of them at the breathtaking speed of some sixty miles an hour. "Little fear that they won't all be tucked up cozily in Wand-seley Hall well ahead of our arrival." The wind that wafted them along at such a smooth pace, and left them completely unaware of any sensation but floating, was perhaps half the speed of the iron horse below them.

It was a lovely sight, and yet the billowing smoke brought back again the horrors of only a few nights ago. His family home in a blaze, their beloved Charlie trapped beyond a wall of fire, himself lying helpless on a lawn strewn with shards of blown-out glass. And yet, all had ended well— as well as any such catastrophe could end. None had been injured seriously; his own bruised, wrenched leg and burnt hand were the worst of the lot. He was thankful that due to the quick action of Hardy and Bracken in directing the servants, many of the most precious family heirlooms had been rescued. The walls would be rebuilt, the rooms filled again with their treasured possessions. And all would go on. One generation unto another. Charlie was safe. Antonia was safe.

He reached out with his unbandaged hand to hold her soft white hand lying on the skirt of her simple traveling gown, the skirt so narrow there must not be a crinoline under it. He smiled at the gentle look she gave him and began, as nearly on key as ever he could manage, the beloved Mendelssohn melody:

"On wings of song—Ah, lightly,
Heart's dearest, I bear thee away:
A nook is beckoning brightly
Where Ganges' waters play..."

"My love, you were thinking of Norwood." Tonia spoke quietly.

"Indeed, I was. I was thinking with gratitude of all that remains, not all that is gone."

She sighed. "A most proper attitude. I am determined to emulate you. It will be marvelous to see what restoration has been accomplished by the time we return. Whenever I think of the blackened... of the chaos, I shall direct myself to think of the order that will be restored." She lifted her chin with determination.

He squeezed her hand. "My brave Antonia."

"I do so wish we could know, though... I so hope it wasn't my carelessness... I can't recall extinguishing my candle..."

"Which undoubtedly means you *did* extinguish it. Anything you do so completely from habit, you would be more likely to recall if you hadn't done it. We are unlikely ever to know. You must put it out of your mind and think of the new furnishings you will choose. We shall bespeak them in London."

Antonia leaned forward and gave him a peck of a kiss. "It will be great fun. All shall be the latest fashion, just as we saw at the Great Exhibition."

Danvers smiled, remembering visiting the opening of the Crystal Palace together just days before they were married. And Tinker finding a murdered body in the bed.

"Ah, perhaps not a bed with a trunk for a headboard." They both laughed when they realized they had spoken together.

"But first I shall visit my dressmaker, and you your tailor, my love." Tonia looked at her unfashionable dress. "I daresay we shall survive in York with what Isabella and Hardy were able to rescue from the laundry room and our hastily ordered wardrobe should arrive from Northampton in a few days. Still..."

The landscape slipped past below them, returning to the green fields of the Yorkshire countryside. Danvers checked his instruments and made a slight adjustment to counteract their westward drift by pulling on the valve ropes—very gently so as not to disturb the wrappings on his hand—and sent them sailing due north.

"York in just over twenty minutes, my dear. If my calculations are correct."

Her answering smile encouraged him to return to his earlier serenade:

Beloved, let us be sinking
Under the shady palm,
The blissful quiet drinking
And dreaming dreams of balm..."

His song continued as patchwork fields with their many shades of green cut occasionally by a meandering dirt road, small farms with clumps of trees around houses and barns, and pastures dotted with cows and sheep, slid beneath then.

"What river is that, my love?" Antonia asked after perhaps twenty minutes.

Danvers consulted his map. "Yes, that's the Ouse. We are very near. A laurel wreath to the first one to spot the Minster towers."

His words barely had time to be wafted away by the breeze when Antonia gave a cry of triumph. "There! I win!" Indeed, her pointing finger directed his gaze to the vast, lavender grey limestone building with its twin west towers capped with mini-spires.

"Well done, my love. You shall look most fetching in your laurel wreath. If only our host has laurels growing in his garden, that is."

In a short time they had flown over the walled city and Danvers focused all his attention on the intricate valving required to maneuver his aerostat to the open field beyond the city wall. A careful survey through his telescope showed Hardy and two other men waving red flags to signal the designated landing site.

Danvers had hoped the landing might be somewhat smoother, but at least the gondola remained upright and in a few moments Hardy was racing across the field to hand Antonia to the ground. "Ah, and right happy I am to see you, m'lord. I trust it was a fine journey you were having?"

Danvers was glad enough of Hardy's babble, which covered his own difficulty in alighting. He was far stiffer and his leg more sore than he would care to admit. He disliked having to lean so heavily on his stick but on this uneven ground he had little choice.

"Charles! You always did insist on making a grand entrance, didn't you? But I'll admit it was a rather spectacular sight." The young man behind Hardy came into focus. Almost as tall as Charles himself, his black hair parted fashionably in the center above sideburns trimmed so as not to cover his clerical collar, The Reverend Frederick William Leighton covered the last few yards of the field with his hand outstretched, his black cassock blowing in the breeze.

Danvers blinked. He had expected to feel nothing but irritation at his younger brother of whom he had seen so little since he had rescued him from numerous assorted scrapes in his undergraduate days at Oxford. But here was a fully grown, mature young man that, except for the clerical attire, he could have seen in his own mirror only a few years ago.

"Frederick. I didn't expect you to meet us."

"The least I could do, brother, when you've come so far to help me. And in such a difficult time." Frederick saw the bandage on Danvers's hand and walking stick in the other, so moved to clap a brotherly arm around his shoulder instead of taking his hand. "Hardy has told me of the events. We gave thanks at Morning Prayers that all were spared."

"Thank you, Freddie." Tonia coming around the side of the deflated balloon gave her brother-in-law a sisterly peck on the cheek.

Danvers was relieved of the necessity of an answer by the arrival of the third person, a man of late middle years and rotund build with impressive, greying mutton chop sideburns. Freddie spoke, "Antonia, Charles, may I present our host, Sir Gerald Wandseley. Sir Gerald, my brother and his wife, Lady Antonia and Charles, the Viscount Danvers," Frederick made the introductions.

The gentlemen exchanged slight bows in lieu of shaking hands. "My wife is most anxious to welcome you to Wandseley hall. Might I suggest we repair to more comfortable surroundings?"

Leaving Hardy and Sir Gerald's groom to bring the aerostat in a farm cart, Wandseley led his guests to his stately brougham waiting at the edge of the field. A few minutes later the fine team of chestnuts swept the carriage and its passengers around the graveled, circling drive cutting through the smooth green lawn of Wandseley Hall and came to a stop at the foot of a curving double stairway. The manor house had been built in the last century in the Palladian style, but Victorian taste had dictated that ivy be allowed to soften and somewhat obscure its pure classical lines, giving it a comfortable look.

Lady Philomena Wandseley, dressed in an afternoon gown of quality, but with a plainness that showed her lack of concern with the latest fashion, welcomed her guests.

"Humber will show you to your rooms," she indicated the butler. "As soon as you are settled do join us in the parlour for tea."

"Thank you, but I should like to visit the nursery first."

If Lady Philomena was surprised at Lady Danvers's reply, she hid it well. "Of course. The nursery is on the second floor, directly above your apartment. Humber—"

"This way, if you please, my lady." The tail-coated butler inclined his head. If he was even more surprised that Lord Danvers chose to follow as well, Humber was far too well-trained to evidence the fact.

After a round of fond embraces from both of his doting parents, the Honourable Charles Frederick was returned to his cot where he had been playing contentedly. "How did he tolerate the journey, Sara?" Tonia asked, brushing his curls with her fingertips.

"Oh, very fine, m'lady. He quite enjoyed the motion of the train," his nurse replied in a tone that said her charge had enjoyed it far more than she had.

"And do you have everything you need?"

The nurse assured Tonia that she and Charlie had every-thing they required and had only to ask the excellent Wand-seley Hall staff for anything they needed, so Charles and Antonia allowed Humber to usher them down one flight of stairs to a spacious apartment with adjoining dressing rooms. A maid with a white lace cap on her blond hair and a stiffly starched apron over her black dress jumped to her feet from where she knelt by the hearth.

Humber turned to Antonia. "Would you care to have the fire lit, my lady?"

"Yes, please. Just a small one to warm the air." Although it had been a sunny day, this room on the north side of the house was quite cool.

Humber nodded. "You may carry on, Polly."

Danvers went directly to his dressing room where Hardy was already returned from his duties with the aerostat and awaiting his master's arrival to make him presentable. With a resigned sigh and doleful countenance the manservant applied a large dollop of macassar oil to his master's black locks, more unruly than ever after their recent singeing, and attacked them with a silver-backed hairbrush in each hand.

Antonia moved to the fire to warm her hands. It had been cooler than she had realized in the aerostat. "Will there be anything else, m'lady?"

"No. Thank you." The maid picked up her coalscuttle and moved to the door. Antonia watched her go. She moved stiffly for such a young girl. As if she were in pain. "Polly?"

The girl turned around and Antonia looked at her for the first time. She was shocked at the lines in the girl's face and the look in her eyes—was it fear?

"Polly, are you all right?"

"Oh, yes ma'am—I mean, m'lady." She took a step backwards and Antonia realized her question had increased the maid's anxiety. She escaped as Isabella bustled in from Antonia's dressing room.

"My lady, it's most regrettable, all your tea gowns —the fire..."

"Did not my teal-green survive, Isabella?"

"Yes, my lady, but it is not so fine—"

"It will have to do." Antonia was accustomed to being the best-dressed lady in any company, but now she would have to put away her vanity and call upon deeper reserves. She would consider it a new challenge. It might be rather fun.

But putting away vanity did not preclude wearing an extra wide crinoline to emphasize the fact that her waist had almost resumed the prescribed formula of "one inch for every year". Nor did it preclude allowing Isabella to arrange her auburn hair with fetching curls at the neckline.

It was clear that the effort was not lost on Charles when he joined her to escort her downstairs. "Very charming, my dear." He bent and kissed her white neck.

A short time later they were gathered in the parlour with its wide French windows looking out over a flagged terrace and an expanse of green lawn beyond. Their hostess sat before a silver Georgian tea service at a round table in the center of the room, ready to fill delicate rose-patterned teacups with a refreshing brew. She offered, among other delicacies, thin slices of buttered bread, and only slightly thicker slices of ginger cake, as well as the *de rigueur* cucumber sandwiches.

Danvers was just settling into a wing-backed chair with wide, scrolling arms when he was jerked to his feet so abruptly he sloshed the tea in his cup.

"So, I see you have decided to do your duty at last, Charles." The words were accompanied by sharp raps of a walking stick on the parquet floor of the hall.

"Aunt Aelfrida, how, er—charming to see you." Charles bowed, spilling his tea a second time.

The Dowager Duchess of Aethelbert advanced across the Aubusson carpet. "Do sit down while you have any tea left in your cup, Charles. Of course you aren't charmed to see me, but that is beside the point. Duty must be done. Family honour must be preserved."

Charles resumed his seat. "I couldn't agree more, Aunt Aelfrida."

"Excellent. I am relieved to hear it." The Duchess accepted a cup of tea and the thinnest of cucumber sandwiches before seating herself bolt upright on a straight, wooden chair. "You will, then, have informed your brother that under no circumstances will you countenance this absurd idea of his living in his parish and becoming some sort of slum priest."

"Aunt Aelfrida—" Danvers began.

But the Dowager Duchess cut him off. "Certainly, a younger son may take Holy Orders. That is quite traditional. And accepting the living of a parish—there is nothing wrong in that. I will even allow it to be useful, what with your hair-brained father going off to Paris and abandoning all family duty."

"Frederick William has an adequate allowance, I can assure you, your grace," Danvers answered stiffly.

Antonia held her breath. Surely even Aunt Aelfrida didn't mean to discuss such family matters in front of their host and hostess?

But the duchess was irrepressible. "Adequate! What is that to a young man of spirit? No, let him take the living and do his duty to make his annual visit to his parish—surely the curate can see to its needs the rest of the time. What else are curates for, I ask you? Cure of souls, that's what the title means—so let the man get about his business with the souls in his care. There is no need for Frederick to be interfering in such matters."

Antonia smiled as she indicated a book of poetry on the table beside her chair. "Ah, *The Temple*; I believe George Herbert is one of your favorite poets, Aunt Aelfrida. So surely you recall that is just what people said of him. The polite world was scandalized then, too, when he took up residence in his parish at Bemerton."

The duchess raised her lorgnette and looked at Antonia as if inspecting something rather unpleasant under a microscope. "And are you, young lady, suggesting my thinking is stuck in the 17th century?"

"Never, Aunt!" Danvers spoke for Antonia. "I am certain I

can vouch for Tonia that the 17th century never crossed her mind."

Antonia's smile broadened. Never by the slightest inflection would he indicate that the family actually found the Dowager Duchess's thinking to be quite medieval.

"Ah, but I couldn't be more flattered than to be compared to Herbert!" The Reverend Frederick William entered the room with a bow to the ladies. He had put off his clerical attire for a well-cut black suit and white shirt, his cravat tied high on his neck with a bow. "Thank you for taking my part, Antonia." He looked at his brother as if enquiring whether he could be numbered among his supporters. Danvers returned his look with a frown.

Antonia moved her skirt aside to make room for the newcomer beside her on the settee. "So must I call you Father Frederick now?" She kept her voice low so as not to disturb the polite conversation swirling around them, and to invite a confidential tête à tête.

"Oh, no. That might be used a little in London, but it's too high for us." His grin was self-deprecating. "Most call me vicar, but Freddie will do very well *en famille*."

"Well, Freddie," she put the slightest emphasis on the name. "You look very well. Very happy." She was convinced Aunt Aelfrida was overreacting. As usual.

"I am. There's the most wonderful work to do." He moved to the edge of his chair and leaned forward in his enthusiasm as if he might spring into action at any moment. "Charles Lowder and his Society of the Holy Cross—perhaps you've heard of them—?" Tonia shook her head so Freddie forged ahead. "They're absolutely splendid. They minister in some of the worst slums London—some so dangerous their bishops won't enter them."

"Freddie! Do you mean to say your work here is dangerous?"

He laughed. "Not at all, I assure you. Unless you count getting pelted with rotten eggs and tomatoes by those who disagree with ritualistic worship."

Antonia gasped. "You don't mean to say that has happened to you? No wonder Aunt Aelfrida objects!"

"No, no. Not here, but it has happened in London. No, I assure you, slum work in York carries far less risk." His face resumed its earnest look, "But no less importance. That's how I came to know Daisy."

"Daisy?" It was impossible to keep the shock out of her voice. Were Charles's worst fears coming true, then? She looked around, but they had attracted no attention.

"The young female I wrote to you about."

"I don't recall you mentioning anyone by the highly unsuitable name of Daisy. Freddie, you can't be in trouble with a young woman of the lower orders?"

Freddie shook his head. "I'm obviously not making myself clear at all. Victoria—Miss Hever, that is—works with fallen women. The Magdalen House Asylum and Refuge for Poor, Degraded Females. Daisy was doing very well, considering her advanced condition. Then Victoria found her dead. Since I first wrote there has been a second. And now Victoria herself has become ill."

Antonia put a slim, white hand to her throat. "Ill? Consumption? An asylum for poor women with tuberculosis?" Tonia was becoming alarmed. She knew far too much about the dangers of consumption. "And you are fond of this Victoria?"

"No, no, Tonia, it's not that at all. I don't even believe in a married priesthood."

This was getting worse and worse by the moment. Perhaps Aelfrida was right. "You've joined some order?" For the first time she noticed the small gold cross on his lapel. "You're not allowed to marry?" She grabbed his hand and lowered her voice to a whisper. "Freddie, you haven't gone over—" she paused. "To Rome?" she ended in a shocked whisper.

"No, no, nothing like that. Strictly good old C. of E. It's all a matter of conscience. But Pusey argues that a celibate clergy can focus their energies more closely on their work and—"

Antonia held up her hand. She understood. Her brother-in-law was of the Tractarian persuasion. Undoubtedly he had been influenced by its leaders at Oxford. And now he was set on emulating the slum priests in London. No wonder Aelfrida was upset. Whatever would Charles say when he found out? She sighed. "Tell me about your work among the fallen women of York."

He turned to her, his face alight. "That is exactly what I had hoped you would say! Lady Billingston, our patroness, is grand. You'll soon see for yourself. She'll be at dinner tonight. She's a baroness, although her husband is plain Mister. I've told her all about you and Charles and the murders you've solved. I told her I knew you could solve this.

"You see, the problem is... these are—er, street women." He lowered his voice and colored slightly. This was not a proper subject for a lady's delicate ears. "Oh, Antonia, it would be splendid if you would help. The police take no interest—"

"Police?" Tonia felt completely overwhelmed. What was he trying to tell her? "Start again, Freddie. Why should the police be bothered that this Victoria has taken ill? I should expect it happens quite regularly to ladies of the night." She refused to blush at admitting she knew of such things.

Frederick looked aghast. "Victoria is not a—a... She is daughter to Sir Reginald Hever."

"Then I don't understand what you want of me. Would

you have me help nurse her? Or take her place with the asylum work until she recovers?"

"No, no. I would have you investigate. Victoria is convinced these women's deaths are not of natural causes."

"You mean to say they've been murdered?"

$\mathscr{H} \quad 5 \quad \mathscr{H}$

Antonia was still trying to make sense of her conversation with Frederick when the gong sounded at eight o'clock and the guests gathered in the withdrawing room. Their host met them and offered drinks.

A short time later Humber announced Lady Carlotta Billingston and her husband. Lady Carlotta, an imposing ramrod straight figure who stood almost a head taller than her husband, swept into the room in an electric blue silk dress trimmed with tasseled braid. The blue of the dress was obviously chosen to highlight her abundance of red hair—which Tonia felt certain was helped to its deep auburn shade by the application of henna. Her husband Sylvester followed in her shadow. Billingston was a small man with a sweeping mustache whose family, Freddie had mentioned, had made their fortune in York's tanning industry in the previous century. His presence was barely noticeable as all eyes turned to the compelling Carlotta.

Antonia smiled as she tried to recall whether she had ever seen anyone upstage Aunt Aelfrida before. Her smile widened as she noted that Aelfrida dealt with the situation by the simple expediency of turning her back on Baroness Billingston and focusing her entire attention on Freddie.

Sir Gerald led the baroness, with her husband trailing behind, across the room to present them to Lord and Lady Danvers. Antonia was surprised that the baroness seemed taken aback for a moment. She suspected that didn't happen often. Lady Billingston's recovery was quick, however. "Allow me to welcome you to our little corner of Yorkshire. I trust your journey wasn't too tiring?"

"Thank you, it was most refreshing," Antonia replied.

Lady Billingston, however, had turned her attention to Danvers. She surveyed his bandaged hand and the stick he leant on. "You have had an accident, Lord Danvers?"

Danvers explained briefly about the fire at Norwood Park. Lady Billingston was aghast, but as she quizzed Danvers about the details Antonia turned from the conversation to accept a glass of sherry from the footman. This was a mistake because it put her in direct line of conversation with Sylvester Billingston. Behind them she heard snatches of Carlotta Billingston soliciting a subscription for the Magdalen Asylum from Danvers while Antonia herself struggled to make conversation with the woman's husband. Her companion, however, seemed far more interested in his glass of sherry than in talking to Lady Danvers, although she did her best to draw him out on the comparative advantages of lambskin and sheepskin for ladies' gloves. For a moment she thought she had hit on a lucky topic when she discovered that his wife's family estate was situated not far from Norwood Park in Northamptonshire, but that soon dwindled as Billingston declared he had not visited his wife's family for many years.

At last the gong sounded again and their host offered his arm to the Dowager Duchess to lead her in to dinner. Charles, likewise, extended his arm to their hostess. Frederick turned to Lady Carlotta, leaving Antonia to be led by Mr.

Billingston to her seat on their host's left. The long oak table in the center of the dusty rose and ivory dining room gleamed with candlelight on silver and crystal. An enormous oak sideboard stood on one side of the room and at the end was a large fireplace where a blazing fire would burn on crisp evenings, but tonight held an ornamental fan.

Humber served the vermicelli soup from a large tureen on the sideboard and a footman handed the plates around. Antonia was more than happy to answer their host's questions about her experiences as the wife of an aeronaut and entertained the entire company with an account of their being blown off course onto the Hebrides on their honeymoon.

When the courses were changed and the soup replaced with deviled whitebait, however, it was time she must turn her attention to Lady Carlotta seated to her other side. At least Carlotta more than made up for her husband's silence with her verbosity. "How long will you be in York?" She enquired.

Antonia explained that their plans were indefinite, as they couldn't return to Norwood Park until the hall had been sufficiently rebuilt. Carlotta was dismayed to hear of their recent loss. "But my dear, how dreadful for you. Lord Danvers did mention he had burnt his hand, but I had no idea." She paused for a bite of fish. "Now, there's only one antidote for your loss. You must have total rest while you're here. Take solace in our lovely Yorkshire countryside. Do you paint?" She didn't wait for Antonia to reply. "Gentle watercolor painting—that will be just the thing. You may safely take my advice, I have had a great deal of experience with invalids."

"I am not an invalid," Antonia managed to say when Carlotta paused for a breath.

"Oh, my dear, of course you are. Your nerves. You have received a great shock. Your condition is most delicate. I cannot imagine what your husband was thinking bringing you into society, but you must take complete rest here."

"Nonsense, Lady Billingston," Frederick flew to Tonia's defense from across the table. "She must throw herself into good works. Work for the poor. Work for God. It's the only solace."

Tonia opened her mouth to reply, but Freddie carried on. "You could be a wonderful help at the Magdalen Asylum. We do a superb work. The women we help aren't evil. Most are simple country girls who came to the city looking for employment and couldn't find it. Many are maids who were taken advantage of by their employers. Perhaps the saddest cases of all are young girls, barely in their teens whose mothers were pr—"

"Frederick!" Aelfrida, sitting next to Freddie, cut him off sharply with a warning tone. "You forget yourself."

Frederick colored above his high, white cravat. "Er— whose parents have died, that is," he finished in a barely audible voice.

An awkward silence hung over the table while the entree of quenelles of rabbit was served. When Humber and the footman had withdrawn, Sir Gerald turned to Aelfrida, obviously attempting to ease the stalled conversation. "I believe we have an old friend of yours coming to stay with us, Duchess. Judge Bramwell will be here for the assizes. He mentioned working with the late Duke on the Common Law Procedure Commission."

"Indeed. It will be quite acceptable to see him. My late husband had great respect for Bramwell's views." The duchess took a sip of wine. "That is excellent news. Baron Bramwell won't allow any of this newfangled psychology mumbo-jumbo at the trials of poisoners brought before him."

Wandseley cleared his throat sharply as the realization struck him of what a wrong turn his conversation gambit had taken. Antonia smiled. How difficult life was for men who had ever to be protecting their wives and daughters from sordid topics such as prostitution and murder. Even the most forward thinking would hardly allow his wife to read a newspaper that he had not censored first for the innocence of its subject matter.

But not surprisingly, Carlotta Billingston was no such shrinking violet. Her reply showed her to be well informed on the intricacies of the cases to be brought before the court. "How interesting that will be. One cannot walk down a street in York without hearing a running patterer recounting the tale of 'poor Harriet poisoned so wickedly by her husband.' They say he's quite insane. Do tell us what you think, Sir Gerald, is Dove mad or bad? Do you think it likely he'll get off by pleading diminished responsibility?"

"My dear, surely—" Sylvester Billingston made a mild protest at his wife's outspoken questions.

But she ignored him as she continued, "There seems to be little question Dove poisoned his wife."

Relief at the necessity of being spared replying showed in Sir Gerald's face as Humber entered with the iced asparagus remove. But it was never served.

A sob from the hall turned all the diners' heads toward the door an instant before it swung open and a maid burst in with tears streaming down her face. Humber took one horrified look at the servant who had stepped so far beyond propriety, but before he could remove her from the room she burst out. "It's Polly. She's dead."

❧ 6 ❧

"See to it, Humber," Sir Gerald growled. "Peter," he turned to the footman still holding a platter of iced asparagus. "Take Suzanna to Mrs. Selby."

Peter looked helplessly at the platter in his hands.

"Leave it on the sideboard and get on!" Sir Gerald's cheeks grew an alarming red under his white muttonchops.

"Perhaps our guests would find a brief withdrawal refreshing." Philomena Wandseley rose to her feet and indicated the ladies should follow her.

Charles smiled as he noted the look on Antonia's face that clearly said she would far rather accompany Humber to the servants' quarters. He turned to their host who was obviously at a loss as to what to do next. "Sir Gerald, perhaps you would like me to accompany your butler? I have had some experience in emergencies of this sort."

Wandseley waved his hand as if in an effort to sweep the whole inconvenient interruption away. "By all means, if you like, my lord. But it's all nonsense. Maid's hysterical. Humber will find Polly in a deep sleep. I should dismiss them both but decent servants are so hard to come by."

Wandseley rose and moved to the sideboard where the crystal decanters of port stood surrounded by short-stemmed glasses. "We might as well..."

Danvers hurried to the door and crossed the hall to the sweeping stairway. He took it as quickly as he could, but his leg pained him sharply and his bandaged hand meant he couldn't grip the rail as tightly as he would like.

The stairway leading from the floor above the nursery was narrow, the treads bare wood. At the end of a hall dimly lit by gaslights on the wall a door stood open. Danvers almost collided with Humber backing out of the room.

The butler collected himself quickly. "I'm afraid Suzanna was quite correct, my lord. Polly indeed seems to be dead."

Danvers stepped around him and stood just inside the doorway. The room was sparse, offering two narrow iron beds, two chests of drawers and two wooden chairs. Presumably Suzanna was the other occupant. Polly lay on top of the bedclothes which were rumpled, but did not appear to have been thrashed about. Except for her unnatural stillness and pallor the girl could be asleep. She still wore her black uniform, but had removed her shoes, cap and apron before lying down. Her hair had come loose from its pinning and splashed across the bolster. Had she taken to her bed feeling unwell and suffered a heart attack?

"Has she been unwell?" Danvers turned to Humber, waiting uncertainly outside the open door.

"Not so as to interfere with her duties. That would not have been tolerated. As to anything minor, Mrs. Selby, the housekeeper, would know about that."

"She appears to have been a healthy young woman. Is there any reason she would take her own life?"

"I shouldn't think so, but our female staff would not confide personal matters in me. It would be most improper."

Danvers nodded. That was quite right. He would need to

talk to Mrs. Selby. He was about to leave the room when he noticed a bottle lying on its side on the edge of the chest of drawers beside a stack of linens.

He picked up the bottle and sniffed the remains of its contents. The pleasant almond smell brought back a cherished childhood memory. As a lad he had often hung around the kitchen at Norwood Park watching Cook prepare his favorite treat—Maids of Honour. When it came time to add the almond flavoring she would draw the cork from a small brown bottle and allow him a deep sniff before adding a few drops to her batter. Twenty minutes later he would be heading for the park with a burning hot tart in each hand.

"I should like to speak to your cook." He brought himself back to present reality.

"That should be no trouble, my lord. Although I won't answer for what state she'll be in after having had her dinner interrupted by such an unpleasantness."

Danvers focused on the stack of sheets and towels. "Surely these don't belong here?"

"No, sir. In the linen room, of course. Perhaps Polly was carrying them to the cupboard when she was overcome."

Danvers considered. "Is the linen room on the third floor?"

"No, sir. Naturally it is on the first floor to be convenient to most of the bedrooms."

"Quite. So if she was carrying the linens up from the laundry when she was taken ill, why not leave them in the linen cupboard on the first floor rather than carry them all the way on up here?"

"Perhaps she felt too ill?"

"Perhaps. Yet she had strength and presence of mind to remove her cap, apron and shoes." Danvers took the sheet from the top of the stack and unfolded it to cover the body. He paused before covering her face.

He had seen death many times in the years since he had first helped his friend Sir John Boileau investigate the brutal murders at Stanfield Hall. Few of them had appeared to be as peaceful, even natural as Polly's. But whether natural or violent he always felt overcome by sadness.

Death was diminishing to all it touched, as well as to its victim. Especially when it visited a young person like the one before him. Only a few hours before Polly had been lighting a fire for his own comfort. He recalled hearing Antonia speak kindly to her; thanking her. But, guilt stabbed him, he had not thought of her as a person. Only in death had he taken time to look closely enough to notice that she had an exceptionally fine head of golden hair. How old would she be? Possibly twenty. Just beginning life. The waste. He let the sheet fall over her face.

"No, I didn't send Polly up to put laundry away. That had been done hours ago. She should have been turning down the guests' beds and making certain the coal scuttles were full for the night." Mrs. Selby sounded outraged that anyone should suggest her housekeeping schedule could go so far awry as to allow seeing to the laundry at this late hour. "I have no idea why the girl would have been in her room. It was certainly not with my permission."

Humber had requested the cook and housekeeper to join them in the butler's quarters off the kitchen. When they walked through the kitchen Danvers had noted a beautifully arranged cheese tray and tall bowls of fruit on the central table which would have been the next courses had their dinner not been interrupted. "Had she been unwell lately?" Danvers asked.

"Not of late," the housekeeper answered. Danvers waited for more, his eyebrow cocked. "A few weeks back she seemed to have a touch of the grippe. Do you recall, Mrs. Foss?" She looked at the cook.

"That's right. Couldn't tolerate her food, so I made a special pot of beef tea. Mrs. Beeton's receipt, of course." She sniffed. "I don't care what that uppity Miss Nightingale says —a good savoury beef tea will set any digestion to rights." She paused and her assurance faltered slightly. "Now that I think on it, though, it does seem that her appetite was a bit off of late. I had to tell her more than once to clean up her plate. I'll not have good victuals going to waste in this house. Not like some fine houses where they don't take no mind to such things. 'Tisn't right, not with so many poor souls going hungry."

Danvers described the bottle that smelled like almond flavoring next to Polly's bed. Without a word, Mrs. Foss strode back into the kitchen as fast as her short legs on a sturdy body would take her and returned in a moment with a bottle that could have been the twin to the one he remembered from his childhood. "There you are. Like that?"

Danvers removed the cork. Ah, exactly as he remembered. "That's it, Mrs. Foss. So what would Polly be doing with a bottle of almond flavoring in her room?"

Mrs. Foss's eyebrows rose to the fringe of her curly red hair. "I'm certain I don't know, m'lord. But this bottle's mine and no doubting it."

"And it's the only one you have?"

"Certainly. What would I be wanting with more than one?" She frowned at him. "Clear glass, you say? Not brown?" She shook her head. "Wouldn't have it. Clear glass lets the flavor evaporate. Brown protects it from light. Who would do such a daft thing as going to all the work to distill flavoring and then not preserve it correctly? I ask you!"

The cook continued to frown. "What size did you say it was?"

"About the size of a drinking glass, I suppose." Danvers indicated a bottle perhaps four inches high.

"Too large. Flavor'll go off before it's done. Only use a few drops. Or dilute it."

Danvers was feeling more perplexed by the minute. "So you make this yourself?"

"And who else do you think would be doing it? Haven't I been cook to Sir Gerald and Lady Wandseley for fifteen years?"

Danvers realized he was dealing with an artist who would require careful handling. "Yes, indeed. And an excellent dinner we enjoyed tonight, Mrs. Foss. The lemon sauce with the quenelles was the best I've ever tasted."

The cook's reply was a mere "Humph," but she looked pleased. Danvers judged it safe to continue. "So you distill your essence from almonds?"

"Almonds?" Her derision showed Danvers how far he had gone wrong once again. "What do you think I'm making—soup? No, I use bay leaves—from the laurel tree in the garden. It's a very precise process. They must be soaked, brought just to the boil, then simmered—uncovered—all night. In the morning I strain them through cheesecloth. But it must be just the right viscosity. Like a sweet sherry. Too thin and you'll not get enough flavor. Too thick and it could make you sick."

"Sick?"

"Well, of course. Almond water can be poisonous."

Danvers was too confounded to form a question. It was Humber who demanded. "Poison! What do you mean, Mrs. Foss?"

"Well, Mrs. Boyle told me it herself—she as trained me to cook. Started out as skivvy, I did, when I wasn't yet twelve years old, and worked my way up. Best way to learn, but I was a natural. A light hand with pastry is something you have to be born with. In Lord Fanshaw's house, and grand it was—"

"Mrs. Foss! The poison," Humber growled.

"Yes, sir. I'm getting there. For Mothering Sunday it was, the parlour maid was going home to visit her mother, as is proper. Kessia was her name. She was a favorite of Lady Fanshaw's so her ladyship gave Kessie a bottle of laurel water to take home to her mother. Kessia's mother give it to her sister, who ran a shop.

"Daft, she must have been because the shopkeeper poured a glass of it for a customer who drank it straight down. A few minutes later she complained of a stomachache and couldn't talk no more. She was dead within the hour."

"Thank you." Danvers dismissed both ladies with a nod of his head. When they were gone he turned to Humber. "You will, of course, want to notify the girl's family. And I suggest you send for the police."

✤ 7 ✤

Antonia and Charles had sat up late discussing Polly's death, but the matter was now in the hands of Sergeant Carlton from the York Police. Sir Gerald had notified Polly's parents and nothing more could be done until the coroner's inquest the day after tomorrow. So that morning, after she had spent a pleasant hour in the nursery with Charlie, Tonia was more than happy to accept Frederick's offer to show them some of the sights of York.

It had begun well enough as Sir Gerald's coachman took them to York Minster before returning to Wandseley hall to drive Lady Wandseley to an appointment. After only a brief view of the Minster's serenely soaring grey stone arches, however, Freddie seemed anxious to move on. The organist was practicing, filling the space with the rich tones of a Bach chorale. A light scent of candle wax and incense hung in the air. Antonia would gladly have spent the morning in such surroundings, but their guide ushered them back out onto the courtyard, past St. Michael le Belfry, the chapter house and other ecclesiastical-looking buildings.

As they crossed Goodramgate the buildings became

distinctly more ramshackle, the pavement more crowded with hawkers and beggars and the air heavier with less pleasant scents and sounds. "Shouldn't we secure a hackney?" Danvers asked.

But Freddie insisted that their tour would be much better on foot, "Unless your leg—" Danvers curtly assured his brother he could manage very well.

A few moments later, however, Antonia doubted the wisdom of the decision as she lifted her skirts and stepped around a puddle, narrowly avoiding a pile of rubbish as she did so. Freddie had warned them that the Bedern was a "hotbed of sin, disease and poverty." But she had been unable to imagine any place so desperate. At least Danvers was carrying his stick, although she ardently hoped it wouldn't be necessary for defense.

"Is it much further, Freddie?" The smell of rotting vegetation, mud, horse-droppings and unwashed humanity assaulted her nostrils. Beggars, ragged children and street women slowed their progress.

"St. Alphege's is just up here, you don't really see it until you're around the corner."

Antonia pulled her skirts closer to her to protect them from grimy walls stained with years of damp and soot, and wished she had chosen a narrower crinoline for their tour. She hadn't realized Frederick, who was striding ahead of her with no thought for the damage to the skirts of his cassock, had taken his task of ministering to the poor quite so literally. "But you said your church was quite new-built. Why ever did they put it in such a dreadful place?" She had been determined to support Freddie in his eccentric ministry, but this was far worse than she had imagined. Little wonder Aunt Aelfrida was objecting so vociferously.

"That's the whole point—to be in the midst of the people

who need us. The rectory is just across the courtyard so we are available at all hours."

Tonia shook her head in dismay. She could only imagine what conditions Frederick and his curate must live in. And what would the church look like? Undoubtedly as squalid as everything else in this narrow street where the upper stories of the buildings overhung the ground floor, blocking out the sun and giving her the feeling they might topple over on her at any moment. The medieval jettied buildings also served to hold in the cacophony of sounds as costermongers called their wares, draymen swore at their horses and women scolded their squabbling children. How was it possible for Frederick actually to live here?

They turned the corner into an even narrower close and Freddie pointed ahead. Antonia gasped and stopped still, causing Danvers, walking a step behind, to bump into her. She simply couldn't believe the vision of red-brick gables and towers patterned with bands of black and yellow brick, a tall spire rising above it all like a finger pointing to God.

"Lovely, isn't it?" Freddie asked. "A student of Butterfield's built it. We think it's as fine as his London churches."

"But I don't understand—in the middle of all this squalor..."

"That's precisely the point. The poor need a vision of God to lift them above their degrading circumstances. They need beauty, peace, harmony in their lives. Where else are they going to get it?"

Before they could answer, Frederick turned to a ragged boy splashing in a puddle with a stick. "Tad, how is your mother? Is she better today?"

The urchin gave a final slash at the muddy hole, spraying the younger children around it and landing a blob of mud—or worse—on Danvers's impeccable coat. "Nah, she's took to 'er bed."

"I'm sorry to hear that. I'll see that someone brings her some broth." Freddie was quick enough to move back before another spray of mud came his way.

Antonia breathed a sigh of relief when Freddie opened the church door and she could escape the filth. And again, her mouth fell open at the vision of light and beauty as sun from the upper windows filtered onto the golden mosaic reredos, and the stained glass made pools of color on the marquetry floor. Gothic arches everywhere pointed upward as if one could see to heaven.

"We want to give people a taste of heaven. They need to have a hope beyond this life. Music, vestments, incense, candles—most can't read, so we show them in other ways."

"And do the poor come to services?" Charles had been quiet for most of the journey and Antonia could only guess what he must be thinking, but now his voice was level.

"Yes, they do. Many of them. After some encouraging. But we have to win their trust first. That's why the work of the Magdalen House is so essential. Come, I'll show you."

"But, Freddie, it's so lovely. Can't we just stay here in the quiet?" Antonia protested.

"Yes, yes indeed. You must come back. Frequently. We have morning prayers and evening prayers every day and Holy Communion—"

"I mean now."

But Frederick had already turned with a swish of his cassock and was leading back toward the door. "We hoped to secure one of the properties next to the church, but the holding company who owns them has a stranglehold on so much of the land. It's iniquitous the wealth the slum landlords make off property like this. And they refuse to make any improvements to better the lives of their tenants." Back out on the street they passed narrow, rotting stairways leading to upper stories where Freddie told them whole families lived in a single room above the pawnshops, gin mills and doss houses —or worse—which opened onto the crowded street with its gutters running with effluent. "We were lucky to secure a property as near as we did. We're only renting. The landlord wouldn't sell. If we could get our own premises we could make more improvements. But we do the best we can."

Antonia put a hand over her nose to block the stench from the gutter, but before they had to go much further Freddie opened a door under a freshly painted sign reading Magdalen House Asylum and Refuge. Even without the sign, Tonia would have guessed they were there because it was the only building in the street with gleaming clean windows. Almost the only building without broken windows.

The room to the left off the hall was a large dining room filled with scrubbed wooden tables and long benches. "We provide two hot meals a day. Sometimes the soup is rather thin—dependent as we are on the charity of others, but it's always hot and the loaves fresh-baked. And we always offer prayers and Bible reading. It's the only spiritual teaching most of them ever get." Frederick led on into a kitchen filling with steam from enormous cauldrons of broth simmering on the Robinson stove.

A sturdy figure with a long white apron swaddling her maroon dress was bent over the oven. She righted herself, an iron tray of whole wheat buns held with an oven cloth. "Lady Wandseley!" Tonia couldn't disguise her shock at seeing their hostess working in a soup kitchen in one of the worst slums in York.

"Why yes. Didn't Frederick mention that I work here two days a week?" She set the hot tray on a wooden counter and inserted another tray of bread rolls. "Of course, my poor efforts are nothing compared to those of our valiant Carlotta Billingston, but I do like to feel I'm making a contribution."

Frederick moved them out of the stifling kitchen and

back into the hall. As soon as they were out of Lady Wandseley's hearing he chuckled. "What she means is that no one can say 'no' to Lady Billingston. She's absolutely fierce in recruiting her fashionable friends to work in the Magdalen House."

He gestured toward a door at the end of the dark hall. "That's where Isa has her quarters. She'll be sleeping now—or drinking, but there's little enough we can do about that."

"Isa?" Antonia asked.

"She's a nurse. Of sorts. Nursed in the Crimea, but hardly up to Miss Nightingale's exalted standards. She's happy enough to occupy our back room, carry slops and open the door to the poor souls who knock on our door after dark. That's as much as we can ask. It seems after dark is when most women are willing to flee the men who beat them in a drunken stupor before collapsing." He shook his head. "We have a small office in there," he pointed to a closed door. "And that's our storage room. Well, it would be if we had anything to store. Seems we use our supplies as fast as they're donated. Faster, really." They peeked in briefly. Antonia only had time to notice nearly empty shelves and a single, tall cabinet in the corner with a variety of bottles behind its glass doors. Freddie turned toward the stairway.

"Now, let me show you our rooms upstairs." The stairway was dark and the treads creaked, but Tonia noted that, although shabby, everything was scrupulously clean. "It's the merest grain of sand in all that needs to be done. But we have made a start."

At the top of the stairs a landing opened onto a large bare room with several iron beds, each bed occupied by a female figure covered with a gray blanket. One woman clutched a mewling infant to her as she struggled to spoon a mouthful of soup into her own thin lips.

"Can't you shut that brat up?" a woman in a bed across the

room demanded. A figure in another bed merely groaned and clutched at her swollen belly. Antonia wondered if she was in labour.

In a low voice Freddie explained, "Betsy's baby came two days ago. She arrived on our doorstep too weak to walk up the stairs herself. The babe is so tiny it's a miracle she's alive —really that either of them are alive. Iris miscarried her baby last week. She lost a great deal of blood. Goodness knows if she'll ever regain her strength."

"Is the other one near her time?" Antonia asked.

Freddie shook his head. "I don't know. She won't talk. Just groans a lot."

Antonia then turned to her right to observe a woman with disheveled brown hair sitting propped against pillows, opening her mouth obediently as a young woman held a spoon up to her. The spoon shook and a few drops of beef tea fell on the coverlet.

"Victoria," Freddie said and Antonia heard the ring of concern in his voice. "What are you doing here? You aren't well—"

The young woman with curling blond tendrils escaping the smooth coils of hair over each ear stood and turned to him with snapping blue eyes in an unnaturally pale face. "And are you suggesting I should leave Verd to starve? She's much too weak to feed herself." She looked beyond Frederick and saw that they had visitors. "Oh," she lowered her gaze. "Forgive me."

"Charles, Antonia, may I present Miss Victoria Hever, one of our most dedicated workers? Miss Hever, Lady Antonia and Lord Charles Danvers, my brother."

Antonia took a step toward Victoria who barely came up to her shoulder. "I'm charmed to meet you, Miss Hever. Frederick has told us so much about the splendid work you all do here." She had been about to say more, but as she spoke she looked across at the woman in the bed. And almost gasped. She had never seen such a deformity. How was it possible for the woman to eat at all with so much of her face missing?

The woman in the next bed coughed and a spot of bright red blood appeared on the white sheet. Tonia turned back to the hall, holding onto the wall for support. Perhaps taking her movement as an invitation to join her, Victoria Hever followed. "Your patient, what is her ailment?" Tonia asked as soon as they were out of hearing.

"Phossy jaw." Antonia looked puzzled and Victoria continued. Her voice was soft and extremely musical, even when discussing such a dreadful subject. "It's a common ailment among women who work in the match factory—from the phosphorus."

Tonia gaped at the idea that such a horror could be described as a common ailment. "Is it fatal?"

Frederick and Danvers joined them and Tonia couldn't help noticing how Victoria's eyes lit up when Freddie stood beside her. "Eventually," Freddie answered. "Madness comes first, then the poor devils die. But Verd isn't here for the phossy jaw. The few pennies she earned in the factory weren't adequate to feed her family, so she..." He ground to a halt, obviously unsure what to say.

Tonia nodded, his embarrassment filled in the gap for her. "She went on the street. But surely she wouldn't have had much success with that disfigurement?"

"For someone with only a few pennies, in a dark alley..." Freddie reddened. "And then there were complications..." He fumbled to a stop. "Tonia, I shouldn't be speaking of this to you. You shouldn't know of such things."

Antonia opened her mouth to protest that his sentiment was quite nonsensical. She was perfectly aware of the vast numbers of poor women who were driven to the streets and that unwanted children often resulted.

But before she could speak Freddie turned to Victoria. "Victoria, I spoke too sharply earlier, but really, you should be in bed. You are ill yourself."

"But these poor women. We have so few workers." Even as she spoke she leant against the wall.

Just then a light footstep on the stairs announced a newcomer. "Ah, Cece," Freddie sounded relieved at the entrance of a young woman who could be Victoria's mirror image except that the soft curls at the sides of her bonnet were slightly lighter and she was perhaps an inch taller. Freddie introduced Victoria's twin sister, Cecilia,

She acknowledged the introductions, then turned to her sister. "I've come to take you home, Vicky. It was very contrary of you to come out today."

"Cece, you know I can't leave these poor women..." It was obviously a long-standing argument.

Cecilia took her sister's arm and led her toward the stairs. "I'll see to them for you until you're better."

"But your prison visiting?" Victoria's voice floated up the stairwell.

"They aren't going anywhere, are they?"

Antonia smiled at Cecilia's common sense even as her mind wrestled with the idea of two such obviously well-bred young ladies engaging in such activities. "Are they parishioners of yours, Freddie?"

"No, no, their father Sir Reginald is an admirer of Lord Shaftesbury. He and his family are of the evangelical party. This is where the two wings of the church meet—in agreeing the necessity of ministering to the poor."

Tonia's eyebrows rose. "You don't mean they are Methodistical, surely?"

Freddie smiled. "Oh, no. None of that. Quite of the established church."

Antonia knew she had much thinking to do. Aelfrida was

certainly correct as to the unpleasantness, unsuitability, even, of Freddie's work. And for gently reared young women to be working in such a place—well, shocking was hardly an adequate description.

Still, the fact remained, that the poor creature in the next room could not be allowed to starve to death. She turned and strode back to the bed, picked up the spoon Victoria had set aside, and offered a spoonful of soup to Verd.

Her patient was unresponsive. She brushed the misshapen blue lips with the spoon, hoping to wake her gently. "Verd, Victoria had to go home. I'll finish giving you dinner, but you must open your mouth at least a little bit."

There was no reply. Tonia shook her patient gently with her left hand. The head with the skeletal exposed jaw fell to the side. Tonia jumped up, unaware of the beef tea spilling over the bed and herself.

Verd would need no more soup.

8

Frederick dropped his face into his hands momentarily, then took a deep, wavering breath and crossed himself. "Good Lord, how can it be? First Daisy, then the other two and now Verd... It's, it's as if our work is jinxed."

"But you said phossy jaw was fatal," Antonia argued.

"Eventually, yes. But Verd came to us for shelter until her child was born. Her three older children had already been taken into the workhouse. We had hoped to help her find some kind of work after her confinement..." He stopped with a sigh and a shake of his head.

A regal figure ascended the stairs. "Lady Billingston," Frederick sounded relieved at the arrival of his patroness. "I'm afraid we've had another unexplained death."

Carlotta Billingston, clad in an only slightly less electric shade of blue than the night before, strode to the bedside and pulled the sheet over Verd's face. Antonia shivered as she couldn't suppress the thought of the already partially exposed skull. "Should we send for Sergeant Carlton?" Tonia asked.

Carlotta dropped the sheet and turned with a swish of her

skirts. "Whatever for? Whether she died from phossy jaw or complications of her condition should make little enough matter to the police." She turned to Frederick. "I know you will see that she and her unborn child have a decent burial, Reverend. That is the best thing anyone can do for her. It's a blessed release—for both of them."

Antonia thought she agreed with Carlotta's no-nonsense assessment, and yet she found it difficult to dismiss Freddie's concern. He frowned as he handed her into the carriage with Lady Wandseley who had finished her volunteer work for the day. "It shouldn't have happened," he protested.

Danvers sprang awkwardly into the carriage beside his wife with an alacrity that spoke his desire to be away from the dirt, disease and death they had encountered. The occupants of the carriage were silent as they rolled through the flat, green countryside to Wandseley Hall. For Antonia the experience had produced one overwhelming emotion in her —a desire to hold her son in her arms.

And apparently it had been the same for her husband because as soon as the carriage came to a stop on the curved gravel drive in front of the fine, red brick house Charles followed her up the multiple flights of stairs to the nursery so closely she feared he might tread on her skirt, his stick thumping rhythmically on each tread.

The sight of their beautiful, chubby boy in his white dress playing happily under the watchful eye of Sara Bevans brought tears to Antonia's eyes. So much danger in the world. So much horror. And yet here all was peace and beauty as if the fall had never occurred. A sinless, innocent world... If only.

"Charlie!" She swept him into her arms. The child gurgled with delight as she whirled him around, kissed him soundly on his soft, plump cheek and passed him to the arms of his waiting father.

"Has he taken the air yet, Sara?" Danvers asked.

"I was just about to take him out, my lord."

"Fine, a stroll in the garden is precisely what we need."

"Are you certain, Charles? Your leg—"

"Is much improved. If I survived that hellhole Freddie dragged us through I can certainly manage a stroll in a rose garden." And Antonia had to admit that he was limping somewhat less. His stick seemed to be used more for effect than for support.

A few moments later Antonia, smiling, walked beside her husband as he pushed their son in the fine wicker perambulator Hardy had secured for them from a shop in York. The sturdy metal handle provided adequate support for Danvers to abandon his stick, and the white eyelet umbrella suspended over the carriage kept the July sun off Charlie's fair head. Roses scented the air. Tonia placed her hand lightly on top of Danvers's. "This is the way life should be. I had no idea..." Images of their morning's experience jostled in her head. She wanted to shut them out, and yet she knew she couldn't. Now she understood Freddie's determination.

"Freddie's work—it's magnificent. And impossible." No matter how much she struggled she couldn't find words to express her feelings.

Danvers nodded. "No wonder Frederick wanted us to see. It's unimaginable. One hears of such things, of course. And applauds the work of reformers like Shaftesbury." He paused. "I must apologize to Freddie for what I thought earlier. But who could have imagined that the young puppy could have grown up into such an ardent improver?"

"I don't think you need apologize. I think he enjoyed shocking you with the truth."

Danvers gave a wry smile. "Yes, but now one feels rather put to it to come up to scratch."

"So you're going to help him?"

Danvers was quiet for some time as they strolled to the end of the garden, the iron wheels of the perambulator crunching on the gravel. "It's hard to imagine why anyone would murder those poor women under his care. Why bother with someone whose circumstances are already so desperate? But it would be a shame if his work were to fail because something was being mismanaged."

"I can't think what that could be. Everything seemed to be surprisingly clean and the food nourishing, if rather spartan. I wonder what medications their nursing includes? Laudanum, purgatives, sedative bromides... If not overseen by a doctor..." Her voice trailed off. It was too much speculation.

By the next morning, however, Tonia had made up her mind. "I shall undertake Victoria's nursing duties until she is strong enough to return," she announced at breakfast. Fortunately Aunt Aelfrida had chosen to breakfast in her room, so Tonia was spared a lecture on the unsuitability of her determination.

"Carlotta will be pleased," Philomena Wandseley said as she poured a cup of tea from the silver pot on the sideboard. "I shall tell Humber to have my carriage entirely at your disposal."

"Tonia, I don't like your going to Bedern unaccompanied. Cutpurses, footpads, beggars—you have no idea who might accost you." Danvers looked up from the perfectly browned sausage he had been attacking.

"I have no intention of going unaccompanied, my love." Antonia tipped her head to the side, making her red-gold curls fall charmingly across her white neck, and gave him her most winning smile. "I am sure Lady Billingston will be delighted to have your help, too."

Danvers snorted, but a short time later he sat beside his

wife as the countryside turned to cityscape and they glimpsed the towers of York Minster beyond the city walls. Once through Bootham Bar the traffic became more congested as costermongers' barrows, carriages, and dray carts jostled to pass in the narrow cobbled streets. Past the Minster, the noise and smells became worse. A cart piled with broken furniture rattled past, drowning out the cry of a rag-and-bone man. At the next crossroads the din was unimaginable as four running patterers, one on each corner, tried to out-shout each other, waving their papers and bellowing: "Dove trial next week! 'Orrid murder!"

"Terrible truth... Witch doctor sets Diabolical Dove to murder!"

"Sorrowful lamentation for a beautiful young wife. Unimaginable torture by monster Dove."

"Schoolmaster says Dove is mad. Can 'e 'ang anyway?"

Tonia slipped her fingers under the ribbons of her bonnet to block the ruckus from her ears. A few minutes later she fled into the Magdalen House as soon as the carriage came to a stop at its door.

The tireless Carlotta Billingston welcomed her new recruits and handed Danvers a large bucket. "The pump is at the end of the street. We will need three bucketsful to fill each soup kettle." She ordered the viscount as easily as if he were her footman.

Antonia only had time to register the consternation on her husband's face before Carlotta turned to her. "A young girl came in this morning with severe cramping. She is likely near her time, although it's impossible to tell with these cases. She begged for a dose of something so she could get back to— work she said, but she's undoubtedly on the street." She shook her head. "Can you imagine? I sent her to wait upstairs, but have had no time to see to her."

Lady Billingston turned to a shelf, selected a bottle

marked cider vinegar and thrust it at Antonia. "Heat a small amount of this with half water. And rub her abdomen with it. See that she drinks an additional two ounces. Undiluted."

A volunteer arrived and began scrubbing vegetables for the soup pot, but before Carlotta could direct the newcomer she was interrupted by women squabbling in the room overhead and Carlotta bustled out. Antonia found a small saucepan for heating the vinegar rub and was soon mounting the narrow, rickety stairs, the prescribed rub in one hand and a glass in the other.

She was relieved to find her patient sitting bent over on a hard wooden chair. She had hoped she wouldn't be in the bed where Verd had died yesterday. "Hello, I'm Antonia. Lady Billingston asked me to see to you. How are your cramps now?"

Tonia was shocked at the childlike face the girl lifted to her. She could hardly be sixteen years old. In spite of the dirt on her hands, her pale blond hair was scraped severely back and her face washed clean. Her blue eyes were surrounded by dark shadows and her cheeks sunken. Her much-patched dress hung on a thin frame with a telltale bump in the front. She looked frightened. "Ah'm better now, ma'am. Ah shouldn't a come. Ah'll go now." She struggled to her feet, but another cramp took her just as she started to stand.

Tonia caught her. "Nonsense, girl. You're not well. Here, you should be in bed." Tonia glanced around desperately. No choice for it but to put her on Verd's bed. She could only hope the sheets had been changed. Tonia all but lifted the girl onto the bed. She was so light it felt little more than putting Charlie into his cot. "Lay on your side, curl your knees up, it will relieve the cramp."

The girl obeyed and instantly breathed easier.

"There now. What's your name?"

"Millie."

"All right, Millie, you must be brave and drink this. Just two sips." She indicated the glass she held. "I'll rub a potion on you to ease your pains. Then you must eat something." She wondered when the child had eaten her last meal. She could smell bread baking in the kitchen below. She would soon have something nice to offer her patient—after the girl drank that vile vinegar. Tonia held the glass to her lips.

"You must stay here until you are better, Millie. You are very weak and it will endanger your child."

Millie struggled to sit up. "Oh, Ah can't, Miss. Joey an' Floss can't take care o' t' others. I 'ave to..." She sank back on the pillow.

"Joey and Floss? They are your brother and sister?" A slight nod told Tonia she had guessed correctly. "Others?"

"Tim, Sukey an' Lettie"

"What about your parents?"

"Cholera took 'em last summer. An' baby Bunty. Ah'm all they's got."

Tonia sighed. "All right. Tell me where you live. I'll see that someone takes them some soup. When you are strong enough to go home you can bring them here every day for a meal."

In spite of her pity, she spoke severely to the girl. "But you must not go back on the street. Do you hear me? It could kill you, Millie." If starvation or disease didn't get her first, Tonia couldn't help thinking.

"Ah didn't!" She looked at the telltale bump under her dress and seemed to realize it needed some explanation. "We was takin' in washing. But it's only a penny a tub. We needed more. Joey sweeps, but 'e's small and t' bigger boys push 'im off the best crossings." A tear squeezed out of her eye and fell on the pillow. "An' now there'll be another mouth to feed. Floss'll be twelve next year. Ah don't want 'er on t' street."

Tonia rubbed the acidic potion on Millie's abdomen, the

acrid scent stinging her nostrils. She smoothed the girl's skirt over her legs, then took the hand, as slight as a child's, and squeezed. She longed to assure the girl everything would be all right. But how could it? What more could this child sacrifice to protect her brothers and sisters? "I'll get you some bread. You'll feel better with food in your stomach."

By late afternoon Tonia was exhausted. Cecilia had arrived just before noon and Freddie shortly after. They and Danvers served soup and bread to the endless line that formed outside the Magdalen House and shuffled in to sit hunched over their steaming tin bowls at the wooden tables. As soon as one finished another took his place. Although the only inmates of the asylum were women in a delicate condition the soup kitchen served all comers.

Tonia carried trays to the women in the upstairs beds, scrubbed tables, mopped the floor and checked on Millie every time her duties took her near the girl's bed. Apparently Carlotta Billingston's vinegar dose was effective—along with a nourishing meal and a sound nap—because when Antonia asked directions so she and Danvers could take food to Millie's siblings the girl got out of bed and insisted on taking them there herself. "Tha'd never find it, Miss. Ah'll show thee."

Tonia filled a crock with the last of the soup and a basket with bread rolls and assured Carlotta Billingston that they would return—although not the next day because they would be attending the inquest into the death of the Wandseley's maid.

Tonia shook her head. The fire at Norwood, Polly's death, Verd's death, Millie's dire straits—when had she ever been so surrounded by destruction, death and disease? She wanted to escape from it all. Find someplace beautiful, clean and safe.

Millie led them out into the Bedern street running with filth. As she moved forward Tonia looked up, as if seeking a glimpse of pure sky, only to be pulled sharply back by Charles. She had narrowly missed having a slop dumped on her from an upper story overhanging the street.

Millie was right. They would never have found the way. She led along a narrow, dim passage, little more than an alley, peopled with beggars and sad-faced children. Tonia stepped around a drunken beggar sleeping in a doorway. A rat ran along the gutter. Tonia no longer gave thought to the condition of her skirts as they crossed a courtyard of filthy cobbles.

Millie approached a building leaning so precipitously Tonia thought surely it would collapse at any moment. The stench of sour drains and a cacophony of harsh voices followed them up the back steps into a honeycomb of rooms. Apparently each room was occupied by a whole family.

Millie opened a creaking door and was immediately inundated by squealing and sobbing children that seemed to be all arms and legs, each one vying for her attention. "Wait, Ah've brought thee summat!" At Millie's words the scrabbling tumble of humanity looked up, saw the fine lady and gentleman, and turned to stone. Five pairs of eyes stared at them, five mouths gaped wide.

"Cor," the oldest boy managed at length.

"You must be Joey," Tonia advanced toward him, but he retreated into the corner, tripping over a wobbly stool in the process. The room, less than ten feet square, had one grimy, broken window with a table under it. Two chairs sat by the table, but one of them had only three legs. An iron bed stood against one wall, pallets of straw and ragged blankets lined another.

"We have soup and bread for you." Tonia took two rolls from her basket and held them out to the smallest girls who must be Sukey and Lettie. They looked at Millie. She nodded encouragement. The tiny urchins scuttled forward, snatched the rolls from Tonia's hands and shrank back.

Danvers set the can of soup on the table and Millie pulled tin bowls and spoons off a shelf. "You'll take them all to the Magdalen House tomorrow for another meal." It was an order.

Millie nodded as if still in a daze at all that had happened. "Ah will. No fear." She paused as if trying to work out what she wanted to say. "Tha's ever so good, sir."

Antonia was silent for much of the carriage ride back to Wandseley hall. At first all she could think of was how she longed for a bath. There wouldn't be time before dinner for Isabella to fill the grand cast iron tub with hot water, but at least she could bring a brass can of steaming water to the marble stand in her room for Antonia to have a thorough wash.

What had they got themselves into? They had come to York for a quiet recuperation. Only three days here and she already felt as if her life had been turned upside down. It was hardly their first time to look brutal murder in the face. It had been the ferocious Stanfield Hall killings that had brought her and Charles together, but then they had been removed from the blood and horror as they focused on the coming-of-age party for their host's son. Even encountering the underworld of Burke and Hare style body snatchers whilst on their honeymoon in Scotland had had none of the grime they had experienced in the last two days. And the bizarre murder of Catherine Bacon in Canterbury seemed almost genteel in retrospect.

She shivered, although the late afternoon was pleasant. Could she face what must be looked at if they were to find answers for Frederick? But then, could she face herself in the mirror if they let him down and the Magdalen House failed?

9

The next morning Danvers looked at Antonia across the breakfast table with concern. "Antonia, are you quite well? This slum work is too much for you. I don't know what I was thinking to permit it."

Her brief laugh held an unaccustomed brittle ring, but still he was glad to hear it. "My love, I am quite well. Yes, certainly the work is too much. For me. For anyone. But I am absolutely determined we must do what we can while we are here. And I trust that helping solve the mysterious deaths—if they are mysterious—will be of help. I can't imagine how Frederick or Carlotta can devote their lives to such—such despair—even Victoria and Philomena just a few days a week... It's little wonder a delicate girl like Victoria would break down."

Their hostess entered the breakfast room and helped herself to eggs and creamed kidneys from the silver dishes on the sideboard before joining them at the table and responding to Tonia's words. "You are quite right, my dear. But I would despair far worse if I didn't feel I was making an effort." She added a dollop of rich cream and a large spoonful of golden sugar to her coffee, then sighed. "Now today we must attend the coroner's jury for our poor Polly. And as if that weren't enough, the assizes begin next Tuesday, and all we will hear then will be of that dreadful William Dove murder trial." Lady Wandseley took a long sip of her fortified coffee.

"There doesn't seem to be any escaping the sordid. But then, one must do one's duty," she concluded.

Danvers turned back to Antonia. "Are you quite certain you wish to attend the inquest today? I must go to give evidence, but you won't be called. Perhaps a quiet day—"

"Doing embroidery?" Tonia finished for him and made a face. "Make no doubt of it, I shall accompany you."

Hardy spent considerable time fussing over Danvers's attire, exerting great effort on brushing a high-buttoned, collared waistcoat and his most sedate frock coat. "Get on with it, man. I'm answering a few questions in a witness box, not attending the Lord Mayor's luncheon."

"Ah, but to be sure you'll be wanting to look your most respectable. Himself the Coroner won't want to be taking evidence from anyone not respectable."

Danvers smiled and submitted. "Brush away, Hardy, although since the inquest is being held at one of the city's more popular drinking establishments, I doubt most sincerely that the coroner will notice." Then another thought occurred to him. "And perhaps, while I'm busy being respectable, you might want to be helping out at my brother's asylum for the distinctly unrespectable."

"Looking to see who did for those poor ladies of the night?"

"We aren't certain they were 'done for,' Hardy, but I know Lady Billingston could use your excellent services."

"And I might just happen to be picking up some information." Hardy's broad smile indicated his approval of the assignment.

In keeping with the gravity of the occasion Antonia and Philomena had both chosen to wear dark dresses and deep-brimmed bonnets that shaded their faces. Although attending legal proceedings was popular among ladies of the upper orders, it wouldn't do to be too blatant about it.

When they drew up in front of *The Sun*, situated just two streets over from the Minster, and Danvers handed the ladies out of the carriage he was relieved to see there were no patterers hawking broadsheets with lurid details of the fearful death of a young girl in a fine house. They were undoubtedly all busy proclaiming William Dove's calumny. Or even that of James Blomfield Rush. Although it had been more than six years since that brutal murderer at Stanfield Hall had been brought to justice with Danvers's help, many patterers still made their living selling broadsheets recounting the gory details of a respectable middle class family slaughtered in their own drawing room.

Inside the all-too public house the smell of beer and tobacco filled the air and the clink of tankards and buzz of conversation made focusing on the dignity of the occasion difficult. The Wandseley Hall party was ushered to a back room, only marginally quieter, but at least free from the interruptions of barmaids drawing liquor. Danvers noticed two other figures at a table in the far corner. A middle-aged couple dressed in severest black of poor quality sat with heads bowed, shoulders slumped. The woman, with wisps of greying hair escaping her bonnet, leaned on her husband for support. Her body shook and she sniffed softly. Undoubtedly Polly's parents seeking understanding as to why their daughter had died.

The coroner entered with a black robe open over his dark suit and took a seat at the table at the top of the room. A clerk sat to his right and a jury of twelve men found chairs around tables to the side. It was indeed fortunate that with all the interest created by the upcoming Dove trial the unexplained death of one small housemaid had passed unnoticed by the general public. It was not unusual for coroner's inquests to elicit such public interest that they could easily become scenes of near brawls.

Indeed, Sir Gerald had told Danvers just the night before that the first day of William Dove's inquest at the Cadogan Arms in Leeds in March had produced such a melee that the proceedings were moved to the Leeds Court House for subsequent days. But nothing like that was likely to occur here, although two men, carrying pots of gin, did wander in and take seats at a table, obviously looking for entertainment to accompany their libations.

Humber was the first to give evidence. Looking distinctly uncomfortable in these unaccustomed surroundings, Sir Gerald's butler swore to give truthful evidence, the stiffness of his spine clearly stating that he had never been anything but truthful in his entire life and having to swear to the fact was highly insulting. His account of the dinner party, of the maid Suzanna's interruption and of his and Lord Danvers's inspection of the maid dead on her bed was precise.

"And you recognized her instantly as the maid Polly Summers?"

"That's right, your honour—"

"I am not a judge, Mr. Humber. You may address me as sir."

Humber nodded. "Yes, sir. Polly had served as upstairs maid for just over three years in Sir Gerald's household."

"Under your charge?"

"My charge and that of Mrs. Selby. The housekeeper has most direct oversight of the female staff."

"And you had no reason to complain of her work?"

"None, you—er, sir. She was a hardworking country girl. They make the best maids—those as are trained by their mothers." That brought a louder sniff from the woman in the back. "You don't get those who have had to scrabble in the back slums when you hire country girls. Not like you do from town girls."

Humber was asked to step down and Danvers was next. He confirmed Humber's account and added more detail to the orderly condition of the body on the bed and the stack of fresh linens and bottle of almond flavoring on the chest of drawers.

"Almond flavoring?" The coroner's eyebrows rose. "And what did you make of that?"

Danvers recounted questioning the cook and the house-keeper about the bottle and the linens. "But I didn't draw any conclusion. I simply suggested Humber send for the police."

"Right, quite right. Thank you, my lord. You may step down."

The earnest figure of Sergeant Carlton, the brass buttons his dark blue uniform polished to a high gleam, was next. Carlton explained that he had been on night duty in the Bootham Bar ward when he was summoned to Wandseley hall. He confirmed the details Danvers had mentioned. "And did you have any reason to doubt that the death was of natural causes, Sergeant?" The coroner asked.

"No, sir. But she seemed a healthy young girl. What need would she have to just lay down and die? What's natural in that, I ask you?"

"I'll ask the questions here, Sergeant."

"Yes, sir. But I mean to say, she didn't look as she'd been ill."

"And there were no signs of foul play? Or indications that she had taken her own life?"

"Well, we didn't find no note. I've never heard of anyone

committing suicide with almond flavoring." That produced a snigger from the drinking men, but Polly's mother gave an outcry. The suggestion of suicide was a serious one, indeed. If that was the ruling, Polly's parents would not be allowed to bury her in the consecrated ground of their village church-yard. Summers put an arm around his wife's shoulder and she stifled her sobs against his shoulder.

The next witness was Hiram Bennett, the medical examiner who had conducted the post mortem on Polly. "And what are your findings, doctor?"

"There was no indication of illness as has been suggested. Polly was a healthy young woman."

"Did you conduct a microscopic examination of the heart, to see if it was diseased?" The coroner asked.

"There was no need to. The deceased had shown no symptoms of heart disease and her death gave no indication of such."

"So your examination produced no information for this court, Mr. Bennett?"

"Only that the deceased was three months with child."

Mrs. Summers gasped and her chair crashed to the floor as she jumped to her feet. "No! That's a lie! Our Polly was a good girl! She weren't like that! She never..." Her words were swallowed in a racking sob as her husband righted her chair and pushed her gently back down on it.

"You are certain, doctor?" The coroner asked.

Bennett pulled himself upright and adjusted the lapels of his coat. "It's not something I'd be likely to be wrong about, sir."

"Are you suggesting that Polly Summers died as a result of being with child?" The coroner made little attempt to keep the skepticism out of his voice.

"Only indirectly. You see, sir, Mrs. Bennett is a fine cook; she put me on to it. It's the almond flavoring—distilled from laurel leaf. Poisonous they are in large dosage. It is my belief that Polly consumed the tincture of laurel leaf in an attempt to get rid of the child, and was unaware of the fact that laurel ingested in that quantity can be fatal."

Danvers turned in surprise as the room behind him filled with excited expressions of prurient outrage. He had been unaware that several more spectators had wandered in from the public room. And they had been well rewarded for their effort. They had the story of a young woman seeking to destroy her unborn child who had inadvertently killed herself in the attempt.

The coroner instructed the jury as to the possible verdicts they could return: Death by natural causes, accidental death, suicide, death by misadventure. It took the jury less than ten minutes to return a verdict of death by misadventure.

Mr. Bennett led his weeping wife from the room.

Danvers offered his arm to Antonia to return to the carriage. They couldn't be free of the hubbub of the public house quickly enough for him. Outside he turned to Sir Gerald. "Lady Antonia and I shall call on my brother. Don't keep your carriage waiting for us." He barely paused for Sir Gerald's reply before hailing a hackney cab. The rhythmic clatter of the horses' hooves on the cobblestones helped to order his swirling thoughts.

Antonia remained silent for the space of the ride to St. Alphege Church, but once inside its well-ordered sanctuary she turned to him. "All right, Charles. I have been watching the energetic churning of your mind with enormous patience. Don't you think it's time you rewarded me by sharing your thoughts?"

He smiled and led her to a pew where the afternoon sun made pools of blue and gold from the stained glass window. "Indeed, you are a marvel of patience, my love. But I don't know that my jumbled thoughts will make much of a reward."

Tonia removed her bonnet and pulled her skirt aside to make room for him to sit closer to her, giving him all of her attention. "Are you satisfied with the verdict, my love?"

"Satisfied? What could possibly be satisfying about it? It tells us nothing. Did Polly truly attempt to abort her child? Did someone tell her that would be the effect of the potion? Or did she drink the tincture by accident attempting some other result? Who was the father of the child? Why didn't the coroner question any of the servants as to Polly's follower? Perhaps they were planning to get married? How did an upstairs maid come by a bottle of laurel water? How—"

Tonia held up her hand. "Gently, Charles. So many questions. Let us consider. We need to know more about the properties of laurel water. What other results might she have expected?"

Tonia ticked the points off on her fingers. "And we definitely need to know who the father was. Had Polly told him —or anyone she was with child? Surely Mrs. Selby would know if Polly had a follower, although she might have gone to great lengths to keep it secret. Many houses don't allow maids to have followers and she would lose her position."

Danvers nodded. Talking to Antonia always helped him see things more clearly. "Yes, we need to know all of that. But most important of all—where did Polly get the fatal extract?"

❧ 10 ❧

"Ah, Charles, Tonia. I didn't expect to see you here today." Frederick, looking pale and strained above the stiff collar of his black cassock, stepped out of the vestry. "Have you come to help? I must say, that's extremely devoted of you. And much appreciated. Victoria sent a note to say that her physician has recommended she take the waters at Harrogate. Sir Reginald has taken both his daughters, so that does leave us shorthanded. I'm just on my way over to the Magdalen now."

Antonia took a deep breath. Time to leave the serenity of the church and enter the world of dirt, crime and poverty. In just the short distance to the asylum, the narrow street teemed with ragged children, women with faces of despair, and crippled beggars selling toys carved of bone and bottles of various concoctions promising miraculous cures.

She considered. Could this be where Polly obtained her laurel water? Had she been sent on an errand for her mistress and spent a penny or two of her own on an elixir to cure her of her troubles? A one-legged man, surrounded by a collection of liquid-filled bottles, leaned against the building, calling. "Mother Maddie's Miracle Tonic, only tuppence. Good for wot ails thee."

"Wait, Freddie. Charles, these bottles—"

Danvers nodded and approached the seller. He purchased a small bottle similar to the one that had been by Polly's bed. He removed the cork and sniffed. Tonia could tell by his reaction that he was not smelling almond. Still, Danvers questioned the man who denied selling a bottle to anyone matching Polly's description.

"There are others, though," Tonia insisted.

"Yes, countless sellers of doses and draughts." He shook his head. "It seems hopeless. Still, I shall set Hardy to enquire."

Tonia breathed deeply as they entered the kitchen of Magdalen House. Four enormous pots of soup simmered on the stove, making the room uncomfortably warm but filling the air with a slightly astringent, aromatic smell, which was a great relief after the stench of the street. "Lady Billingston, you have outdone yourself. What an appetizing aroma."

Carlotta Billingston gestured to a broad-shouldered woman wielding a large wooden spoon. "I felt the services of my cook were more needed here today. Mr. Billingston can make do with cold roast and salad or dine at his club, as he pleases. Mrs. Elton brought a quantity of bay leaves from our garden to flavor the soup."

Tonia was all attention. She knew little of horticulture, but she was certain that bay was a form of laurel. Could it be toxic? Was it possible that the answer to the unexplained deaths at the asylum was as simple as over-flavored soup?

She moved closer to the cook as Carlotta continued with directions for Danvers and Frederick, sending them to assist the bustling Hardy who was preparing the dining room for the hungry hoard that would soon descend upon them. "Mrs. Elton, you seem to have used your herbs to good effect."

"A bit of flavor in an invalid's broth never did no harm to my way of thinking."

"Are you quite certain? It isn't possible that bay laurel could cause—er, side effects?"

Mrs. Elton glared at her through the rising steam from the pot she was stirring. "And what side effects would that be?"

"I don't have the least idea. It's just that I've heard that too intense a concentration of laurel water can cause—um, weakness, indigestion..."

Mrs. Elton squared her shoulders, withdrawing her spoon from the pot. "Tosh! Your muddle-headed informant must have been confusing bay laurel with cherry laurel. I can't think who would be so daft."

Antonia retreated a step out of the range of Mrs. Elton's spoon and cast about for a safe way to elicit more information. Lady Billingston's cook was obviously well versed in the matter of herbs, and Tonia would like to know more. Ah, perhaps that was her answer. "What useful information, Mrs. Elton. It's apparent you know a great deal about herbs. It's just that my maid has been suffering from indigestion. I would like to know what to suggest to my cook."

Tonia smiled as the spoon returned to the soup pot and Mrs. Elton's shoulders relaxed. "Well, then what you want is *laurus nobilis*. Fierce bitter herb, but fine medicinal attributes it has: I use it regular to treat poor appetite. Won't have any poor eaters around me. What's the use of cooking if people won't eat? That's what I say."

"Indeed, Mrs. Elton. *Laurus nobilis*. I shall tell my cook."

"You won't go wrong. It cures indigestion, colic, gas, dandruff, rheumatism, sprains, bruises..."

In the room beyond, Frederick opened the front door and the hungry of Bedern moved forward to be served tin bowls of Mrs. Elton's herbed soup. No more talking was possible as all the workers' attention was needed ladling soup and serving bread. But Antonia's mind was busy sorting the information she had gleaned. It seemed there were three kinds of laurel growing innocently in common kitchen gardens. Varieties whose use could range all the way from medicinal cures to useful flavorings to poison.

Did Polly's death come down to a matter of the merest mischance? Had someone plucked leaves from the wrong plant, meaning to aid her in getting over the indigestion Mrs. Selby had mentioned? Or did someone—or Polly herself—attempt an abortion that went sadly wrong? Or did someone —perhaps the father of the baby—seize a ready method of ridding himself of an inconvenience?

And could this explain the deaths of Daisy, Verd and the others who had died under the roof of the Magdalen House? Could a less knowledgeable cook than Mrs. Elton have made a disastrous mistake in flavoring their soup? Or had these desperate women taken some such concoction on purpose to end their pregnancies?

Or the barely competent night nurse Isa. Had she emerged from her back room, perhaps gin-soaked, and administered a lethal dose to one of her patients?

Antonia's mind was still running in those lines as she watched Hardy scrub the now-empty cauldrons with water Charles and Freddie had brought from the communal pump and Mrs. Elton heated on the stove. None of those explanations would apply to Verd. Tonia had held the broth herself. It had no scent of bay, and Verd had been far too weak to administer any such potion to herself.

Surely Freddie was wrong in his suspicions of foul play.

His concern for the success of his work had made him overly apprehensive. Considering the dirt, disease and deprivation of Bedern the wonder wasn't that people died unexplained, but that anyone stayed alive here.

Back at Wandseley Hall that evening Antonia and Charles again took refuge from the turmoils of the day by walking Charlie in the garden. At least they began a stroll until Tonia realized how heavily her husband was leaning on his stick. "Charles, is your leg paining you again?"

"It's nothing." The sharpness in his voice and the lines in his face were at odds with his hearty words.

Antonia lifted a hand from the pram and placed it on his arm. "My love, I thought the wound almost recovered. This was supposed to be recuperation for you. You have allowed Frederick to work you far too hard."

Danvers shifted his stick to carry it under his arm in a demonstration of its superfluity, but his next step resulted in a near-stumble. Tonia grasped his arm with both hands and steered him to a bench beside the path. "We can enjoy the view of our son in his pram far better sitting beside him than strolling behind," she declared. "Besides, I want to tell you what I learned today while you were lugging great cauldrons of soup and buckets of water about—which can't have done any good to your burnt hand, either."

She outlined the various types and uses of laurel leaves. "So, do you think it's all a matter of accident?"

Danvers considered for several moments and Antonia noticed the signs of strain in his face relax as he sat. She reached over and took his hand, still wrapped in bandages from his burns. She held it lightly, waiting for his answer. At length it came. "Accident or ill-will or natural causes or something entirely different... It's impossible to say about the Magdalen women. And it might not be the same for each one. The whole thing is desperately sad, but so far I've seen little that we can do about it other than being what support we can to Freddie." He paused before continuing. "About Polly, though, I would like to know who, if anyone, knew about her condition. Most of all I'd like to know who the father was."

Antonia mused, "Peter the footman seems an obvious suspect. He's certainly good-looking enough. And full enough of himself to think any young girl should be his by rights."

"Yes, but he also struck me as being ambitious. He would know that getting mixed up in anything like that with a maid could quell his chances of advancement."

Tonia raised her eyebrows. "All the more reason he might take steps if anything awkward happened." She interrupted to shake a silver rattle to amuse Charlie, then placed it in his chubby hand when he reached for it with a gurgle of delight. "Humber is far too aware of his dignity for anything sordid. I don't think the boot boy ever gets upstairs where Polly worked..." She continued thinking through the male residents of Wandseley Hall.

"Nor was Polly likely to have had much contact with the outdoor staff, although the groom appears to be a sturdy fellow."

The evening air, softly rose-scented, seemed to carry their unspoken thoughts as Antonia hesitated to mention the obvious. "Sir Gerald..." She ventured at last.

Danvers nodded. "I suppose it must be considered. Plenty a lord of the manor considers the female staff his property, and Polly was an attractive girl."

Antonia considered. "Sir Gerald seems to be the epitome of respectability. Still, one never knows. He and Lady Wandseley don't appear to have any children. Do you suppose it could have been a desperate effort to produce an heir? Perhaps with some idea of adopting the child later?"

Danvers pushed to his feet, still favoring his right leg. "I'll ask Hardy to make discreet inquiries among the staff. And find out about frequent male visitors to Wandseley Hall, as well."

❧ 11 ❧

"Paining you still, is it, m'lord?" Hardy asked the next morning as he prepared to apply strips of linen spread with a liniment of equal parts lime-water and linseed-oil to the remaining fluid-filled blister on Danvers's right hand. Without waiting for a reply he continued, "If pain remains after a week a powder of mercury and chalk is for being just the thing—"

Danvers gave a sharp guffaw. "Hardy, you missed your calling. You should have been a surgeon. Just wrap the blasted thing and get on with it." He held his hand out impatiently. "Now, tell me, did you learn anything below stairs last night?"

"Suzanna was right shocked that I should ask about Polly having a follower. Seeming it is that Mrs. Selby is fierce on the subject. Polly would have been given a warning if she had so much as been observed chatting with a delivery boy."

"Hmm," Danvers thought. "That does rather narrow the field if Polly had no outside contacts. I don't suppose she had gone home for a visit? Mothering Sunday, perhaps? She might have had a beau in her village." He counted on his fingers, then shook his head. Mothering Sunday had been in early

March this year. Polly would have been more than three months gone if that was the answer. "What about her half days off? Did she visit anyone? Could she have been meeting anyone?"

"To be sure, I'll enquire, m'lord."

"Fine, Hardy, and if one of Sir Gerald's carriages could be at our disposal, I'll have you drive Antonia and myself to that vexatious Magdalen House. That's the trouble with do-good-ers, they aren't happy keeping all the glory for themselves, they have to put everyone they meet to work. And Antonia will not be persuaded to stay away. But you may have the honour of earning stars for your crown by carrying the buckets of water today." He paused, then finished with a note of irony, "I think I'd have preferred it if Frederick had been involved in something scandalous."

He meant it merely as an expression of his irritation that Antonia had been drawn into this unseemly work—and his impatience at his infernal slowness to heal from his burns. But once he heard his own words he caught his breath. Fred-erick? His brother was a frequent visitor to this house. In spite of his fine words about believing in the celibacy of the priesthood—silly Romish idea, to Danvers's mind—could his brother be slaking his natural urges somewhere? Could Freddie have been the father of Polly's baby? And then wanted to destroy it to preserve his reputation and the whole matter gone horribly awry? Or could the rogue have rebuffed her so harshly she took her own life? In his wilder, undergrad-uate days, Danvers might have thought Freddie capable of such behavior, but surely not now.

The thought, however, opened before him a gaping pit of snakes. Was it possible his younger brother shared their father's rapacious appetites that had caused him to take up residence in another country? The other women in Freddie's parish... If they then came to the Magdalen House for asylum... But no, that didn't make any sense. If Freddie had a hand in any such he would hardly have begged Charles and Antonia to come investigate. That would have been the last thing he would have wanted.

When they arrived at the refuge some time later, they found that the indefatigable Carlotta Billingston, leaving nothing to vicissitudes of volunteerism, had provided herself with the services of three of her household staff, again including the excellent Mrs. Elton, so Antonia busied herself directing Danvers in preparing trays for the three women upstairs who were unable to come down for their food. Hardy, who had stabled the carriage in a nearby mews, joined them in time to carry two trays, while Antonia, determined to shield her husband, insisted on carrying the third.

Their entrance interrupted Iris's continuing whinge about the tiny whimpers from the infant who was trying desperately to suck a few drops of milk from Betsy's flaccid breast. Nan groaned and clutched at her belly, which seemed even larger than before, but she sat up readily and fell hungrily on the tray Hardy offered her. Danvers turned to the whining Iris, whose complaints stopped as soon as Hardy set the next tray on her lap. Tonia noticed with amused gratification her husband's surprising gentleness in fluffing the sour-looking woman's pillow and helping her to sit up.

"Go on then, wha's a fine gen'lman like thee doin' 'ere? Satisfied art'? It's thy lot wot gets the likes of us in 'ere. Tha's all got appetites tha fine lady wives don't know nowt about. So wheer wouldst'a be if it wer'na for us to satisfy thee? That's wot Ah wants ta know. But then who cares a toss when we gets knocked up? Throwaway—that's wot we are. No better than tha dirty laundry. Not as good. At least tha washes that."

Danvers regarded her silently for a moment, as if considering, then turned and limped from the room.

Tonia turned to Betsy who was struggling to comfort her infant. "Here, let me feed you. You must eat all you can so you'll be able to feed your baby."

The girl raised blue eyes to her, shining with gratitude. "She's so tiny and I've so little to feed 'er."

Antonia was moved by the soft caress in Betsy's voice when the young mother looked at the tiny scrap in her arms. "What is her name?"

"Annie. Annie Rose. Because she's like a tiny rosebud."

"A lovely name. You must eat so you can make more milk for Annie Rose." She lifted a spoon to the girls' lips. Betsy ate hungrily.

Danvers returned, carrying a warm, damp towel. Silently he took the spoon from Iris's hand. From the corner of her eye Antonia watched in amazement as he washed the woman's face and hands. "Cor, whatcher playin' at? Ain't no one never done that ter me." Her words were accusing, but her voice held a tone of amazement.

"Don't ever let anyone tell you you're less valuable than dirty laundry, Iris. You're a human being. Don't forget that."

She gave a cackle of laughter. "Tha's wot the rev'rnd's allus sayin'. 'E's kind, too. Not like that sour little man wi' t' beady eyes." She bit hungrily on the soft, warm bread roll Danvers held out to her.

Antonia was able to coax Betsy to finish a second bowl of soup and to eat three bread rolls. By the time the mother was satisfied, her baby was dozing in her arms. Tonia picked up her tray and tiptoed from the room. Iris's complaints seemed silenced for the moment and Nan wasn't even moaning.

Back downstairs, Tonia was about to congratulate Danvers on a job well done when she looked around the roomful of ragged humanity, working greedily at their meager rations, and realized that she had not seen Millie or her brood of siblings since the girl had promised to bring them in regularly to be fed two days ago. Had Millie's pains returned so severely she was unable to bring the children in for food? Or even to send one of the older ones for help?

She described them to Carlotta and to Hardy, but no one recalled serving a family of six children recently. She turned to Danvers and smiled to see that he was already ladling soup into a large crock. Tonia likewise began filling a basket with bread rolls. "Do you think you can find the way?" She asked.

"Not the way Millie led us, but if we go out to Andrewgate and up Bartle Green I fancy I can locate it. I noticed we were only a few alleys away from the Minster."

Hardy shook his head. "Desperate area. I'll just be borrowing this, Mrs. Elton," he selected the heftiest of her wooden spoons from the crock on the sideboard and brandished it like a cudgel. Frederick took the soup from his brother's bandaged hand and the delegation set out.

After they had turned two corners and headed north Antonia was astonished to realize they were so near the Minster. Magdalen House and its inhabitants seemed a world away from those serenely soaring arches and pinnacles. As they neared the close the streets became even more crowded with tattered children hawking ribbons and various gewgaws, old men offering matches, women with meat pies of every assortment. And the cacophony of the cries of the sellers increased accordingly until Antonia's head was ringing.

She was almost glad to cross into a darker, narrower street to get away from the crush, although the stench of the refuse piled against the buildings was nearly overwhelming. Who would have imagined that rotting cabbage could smell that bad? She looked in some amazement at the building beside her. In spite of the soot and grime covering it, she could see that beneath the filth was a fine stone building, its gothic, leaded windows, although unwashed and broken, still pointing upward above the soil surrounding it.

"Old refectory," Freddie supplied in answer to her unasked question. "In medieval times it was part of the school for the vicars choral of the Minster." He looked around at the dilapidated buildings opening onto muddy streets. "This whole area was their college. The name Bedern actually means 'house of prayer.' It all fell into disuse after the reformation. Now the refectory's a tenement house for Irish immigrants."

Tonia's mind boggled. How many people must be living in there? Likely without heat in the winter. Only a communal oven at the end of the street to cook for their families and a pump just a few feet from the open midden for their water. "Who owns it? Can't they do something?" Tonia asked. Surely some of the desperation could be relieved with a few conveniences.

Freddie shook his head. "Slum landlord. Perhaps same as owns Magdalen House, who knows? People can't afford to pay more for their few square feet of shelter, so why bother improving it? No need for the landlords to cut into their fat profits as they see it."

"Freddie—" She started, but couldn't think of words to tell him how much she admired his efforts. To be fighting such an onslaught of evil—for surely such filth was no less— was an unimaginable calling.

It took some doing—one broken stairway looked much like another—and the warrens of Bedern were full of them— but eventually Danvers found the right one. Antonia thought the muddy cobbles with the overflowing midden across the courtyard looked, or smelled, familiar. She wasn't sure, however, until she saw a thin blond girl leading two littler, even more gaunt children back toward the building. "Flossie?"

The girl looked up with fear in her eyes, like a startled rabbit that would dart into the nearest cover. Then her mouth curved into a smile. "Ow, it's t' soup lady!" She looked at the slightly older of the two girls. "Sukey, run tell our Millie t' lady's 'ere."

Sukey skittered up the stairs and the others followed. "We didn't see you at the soup kitchen after Millie promised you'd come." Antonia said.

"'S Millie, she's took poorly." Flossie's words confirmed Antonia's earlier fears.

In the room, which seemed even darker and more stifling than on her first visit, Antonia saw Millie curled in a wretched ball on the single bed. Joe, the older boy sat in the middle of the floor, attempting to entertain his tiny brother Tim with a game made up from sticks and stones.

Danvers and Hardy set about feeding the children while Tonia tended to Millie. "Is it the cramps again?" Could the girl be in labour, she wondered?

Millie nodded. Tonia felt the girl's abdomen through her thin dress. She couldn't feel the muscles tightening in contractions, but what did she know? She who had been coddled throughout her confinement and, following the fashion set by Queen Victoria, had had a breath of 'blessed chloroform,' as the queen christened it, to dull the pains of childbirth.

"Millie, you must come back to Magdalen House with us. You must have care."

Millie grabbed a bar of the iron bedrail as if to prevent herself being removed bodily. "No. T' others— wots ta become of 'em?"

Antonia knew better than to suggest an orphan asylum or workhouse. Although she had little knowledge of such things, Frederick, in his enthusiastic way, had spent some effort to educate her and Charles. Many orphan asylums were reputable establishments, some even with royal patronage, but many others were places of abuse. And the workhouses were worse, where workers of all ages were treated as less than human, made to labor long hours under terrible conditions for little wage. She followed Millie's gaze as it came to rest on five-year-old Sukey. No, there had to be a better answer.

She turned to Freddie. "We must do something. Millie needs care and she won't leave the others—although she's little enough use to them here as she is. Still, she would fret herself more ill than she is if they are uncared for."

Frederick looked helpless. Another of the unsolvable problems a slum priest was faced with every day. And then his face relaxed into a smile. "School," he said. "Sukey and Lettie are young, but perhaps they will take them with the older ones to look out for them." He turned to Millie. "The Industrial Ragged School is very near Magdalen House. You wouldn't be far from them and they would be learning their letters as well as receiving care."

A spasm crossed Millie's face as another pain seized her. When it had passed she nodded weakly.

"Hardy, fetch the carriage. Millie is in no condition to walk," Danvers ordered.

Antonia helped the children gather up their meager belongings as soon as they had finished their soup and bread. Danvers suggested he and Freddie settle the children into the ragged school while Antonia made Millie as comfortable as possible in the asylum.

Danvers and Freddie set out with the children, Freddie carrying little Sukey. As soon as Hardy returned with the carriage he carried Millie down the stairs.

The iron bed with its solitary grey blanket of the Magdalen asylum looked spartan enough to Antonia, but compared to the broken pile in the miserable room Millie had been in, Tonia knew it probably seemed luxurious to her charge. "I'll bring you a nice chamomile tisane, Millie, and then you must try to sleep."

The girl looked at her with trusting eyes and nodded. Already Antonia thought she saw more color in the girl's cheeks. Surely simply being relieved of the strain of taking care of five young children would be restorative. "Now you must not worry about anything. Your brothers and sisters are in a perfectly safe place. Absolutely no harm will come to them."

The words rang in Antonia's own ears as she descended the stairs. *Please, God, let it be true.*

❧ 12 ❧

anvers couldn't suppress an ironic smile at the picture they must have made. A tall man of aristocratic bearing in a black top hat leaning on his walking stick as he made his way over slick cobbles, and an earnest young vicar in a black cassock that was becoming more soiled around the hem with every muddy alley they crossed, shepherding five urchins carrying assorted bundles clutched in their thin arms. It was enough to make him want to burst out with "Let us Take to the Road" from the Beggar's opera. "*Fill every glass...*'" He began, then thought better of the influence such an outburst would have on the tender charges under his care.

Freddie led back across Bedern toward the old home of the vicars choral, then turned to the right toward Goodram-gate. He pointed to a long, low stone building that looked on the verge of crumbling. "That was the chapel of the vicars choral. Some sort of a warehouse today, I believe."

Danvers was glad his brother knew where he was going because he doubted that he could find his way through this maze alone. Until they rounded another corner and the towers of the Minster peeked above the ramshackle rooftops of Bedern, giving him his bearings once again. Frederick led up to a two-story grey stone building with a massive black door. The sign over the door read York Industrial Ragged School.

At Freddie's third insistent knock a middle-aged woman in a soiled, long white apron over her grey dress, her hair tucked haphazardly in a mob cap, yanked the door open and glared at them sourly. She recovered herself, however, when they asked for the director of the school by name. "Mr. Pimm? Yes, sir, 'e's just come back with 'is roundup of orphans. Spends every day searchin' t' alleys and back streets, 'e does. 'E's that concerned for the poor 'uns. A saint, 'e is. I allus tell 'im." She stepped back from the door. "If tha'll just wait." She bobbed a curtsey and disappeared into the recesses of the building.

A short time later they were joined by a rotund, balding man with a florid complexion made brighter by his startlingly red waistcoat. "Ah, vicar," he sketched a nod in Frederick's direction, then made a deeper, if somewhat unsteady, bow in Danver's direction as he obviously calculated the fineness of the cut of his coat. "My lord. 'Ow can yer 'umble servant be of service?"

Frederick urged the children forward from the shadows. George Pimm patted each one on the head. "Room?" He replied in response to Fred's query. "A'course we 'ave room. Allus room. Can't 'ave 'em on the street. Not at all the thing.

"If yer lordship will be so good as to step this way." Pimm led into a dim office and opened an enormous ledger sitting on the corner of his desk. He opened it and dipped a nib pen in a bottle of ink. "I'll just enter their names in the school list. Very h-important, you understand. George Pimm keeps scrupulous records, anybody will tell you."

He entered each name as Freddie pronounced it, blotted

the ledger, closed the book with a snap and turned to bellow into the shadows behind him. "Louisa!"

"Wot?" The maid reappeared from a side door. "Do'st want tha supper burnt? Jest keep on interruptin' me if that's wot tha's after."

Pimm curled his lips in a smile that pushed his mutton-chop whiskers further apart and emphasized his florid complexion. "My little chickadee, I'm certain you can manage to show these little angels upstairs before returning to the succulent repast we all know yer preparin'."

He turned back to Freddie and Danvers. "I'm sure you fine gen'lemen will h-uxcuse me now." He offered a deep bow that made him appear in danger of falling over. "I have one more section to teach. They'll be h-awaitin' me in the school-room. And eager learners they are, too." The sound of scuf-fling and the thump of something heavy falling on the floor emitted from a room across the hall. "You see, they're that h-impatient for their lessons, they are."

"What is your curriculum here?" Danvers enquired.

"Work and learn, work and learn. We keep a balance. Each child is taught a trade along with their readin', writin', reckonin' and Bible. I'm sure you'll be gratified to know, vicar, each section closes with a ten minute service and prayer. I'm a God-fearin' man, don't you worry."

Back out on the street Danvers frowned. "Did you smell something odd in there?" He raised a white linen handker-chief to his nose. "It was enough to make this putrid fug of Bedern smell sweet."

Freddie shrugged. "Afraid I've been here long enough to be rather desensitized. One open sewer is much like another. I'll wager the frightful Louisa was cooking cabbage."

"Hm," Danvers wasn't convinced. Dead rats under the floorboards might be closer to the mark. "Who oversees the school? The city corporation?"

Freddie stepped around a pile of discarded rags, then jumped aside when the bundle righted itself to hold out a filthy hand. Freddie fished in his pocket and produced a penny.

"He'll spend it on drink," Danvers commented.

"Good. I hope it'll be enough to give the poor devil a few hours of oblivion." They went through a narrow passageway with sooty brick walls on each side and cobbles dotted with horse-droppings underfoot to emerge onto Goodramgate.

"About Pimm," Danvers prompted.

"Oh, yes. There is a corporation, yes. Pimm's parish beadle, employed by the church. As schoolmaster it's his job to keep the streets clear of orphans, waifs and strays."

"If one can credit Louisa's testimony he seems to be assiduous about his duty."

Freddie nodded. "He should be. The church pays him well enough for each child he houses there. Our little donation this afternoon represented a tidy profit."

"Yes, I thought I saw the flicker of greed in his eyes. Along with smelling the gin on his breath."

"Well, hopefully Millie will soon be well enough to look after them again. Although I don't know that that would be a better circumstance." Freddie shook his head. "Despair isn't a Christian response. We know we always have hope. But sometimes..."

13

"Well, I must say it's high time you saw fit to present yourself. But what condition do you call this?" The Dowager Duchess of Aethelbert tapped her walking stick on the red and ochre tiles of the Wandseley Hall entrance even before Humber could close the door behind Danvers and Antonia.

Danvers looked at the splashes of grime clinging to his trousers and knew Antonia's skirts could have fared little better. "With your leave I shall go make myself presentable, Aunt Aelfrida." Danvers handed his hat to Humber, but retained his walking stick as the day's exertions were making his leg throb more than he cared to admit.

"See that you do. Baron Bramwell is one of my oldest friends and was one of the most respected Queen's Council in London until he became a judge this year."

Danvers bit his tongue to prevent himself enquiring whether Bramwell had lost his respectability when he became a judge, but the Dowager Duchess left no room for levity. "I will not be disgraced by my relations."

"Indeed, Aunt Aelfrida, I shall do my best to uphold the family honour."

Lord and Lady Danvers were just going into their rooms to submit themselves to the ministrations of the excellent Hardy and Isabella to repair the ravages of the day, when they met Nurse Bevans on the landing with the Honourable Charles Frederick ready to take his evening stroll in the garden. Tonia scooped him into her arms and stroked his round cheeks and plump hands. "Oh, Sara, I saw the most pitiful case today, it fairly broke my heart. An infant whose mother doesn't have enough milk to feed her. I wish I knew what could be done."

"Pap, m'lady," Sara said.

"I beg your pardon?"

"Feed the infant pap. Mix bread and water with a little sugar. Make it thin-like so you can drop tiny spoonfuls into the babe's mouth. You can add milk later, but not until she's as old as Master Charlie. It'll cause colic if milk's added too soon.'

"Sara, what a treasure you are! I shall see that the mother begins tomorrow." She kissed her cooing son, passed him to his father for a quick cuddle, and both Lord and Lady hurried on to pursue their toilette.

By the time the dinner gong sounded less than an hour later even the most careful scrutiny through the Dowager Duchess of Aethelbert's lorgnette could not have revealed cause for discredit as Charles, with a black satin cravat expertly tied above a silk waistcoat and slim-cut twill trousers escorted Antonia in a newly purchased gown of white muslin trimmed with bands of emerald green satin and bobbin lace into the drawing room.

"Ah, Lord and Lady Danvers, a great honour I have to present Baron George William Wilshere Bramwell. Just arrived in York for the summer assizes." Sir Gerald introduced his guest. The gentlemen exchanged bows and Bramwell bent low over Antonia's extended hand.

"Big doings at the Castle tomorrow. Whole city's agog over this Dove affair, Judge," Wandseley continued.

"You must tell us what to expect, Baron." Aelfrida, splendid in a high-necked lilac silk and lace gown with ropes of pearl adorning her chest entered the room. "I've spent all afternoon reading the broadsheets my maid procured for me and I must say, this is certain to be most entertaining."

"Broadsheets? Surely not, Aunt Aelfrida." Danvers knew it was quite the thing for ladies of fashion to send their servants for such reading material, but only one as outspoken as Aelfrida would admit to it.

"And why not, I ask you?" She rounded on him. "How else am I to keep up on the tittle-tattle? You're not likely to tell me."

"Certainly not." Danvers had hoped to query Sir Gerald about the suitability of Pimm as a schoolmaster. As a local magistrate he would know if any complaints had been brought against the establishment. But it was clear that the trial of William Dove would be the topic of the evening.

And Aelfrida seemed to be the best informed of the company. As soon as they were seated at table Humber handed around the plates of cucumber soup and the duchess regaled them with her views on the family background of the accused. "Most respectable working class stock. Three generations quite successful in the leather-dressing trade, apparently. But it's little surprise that overindulgence in all that Wesleyan Methodism would lead to instability."

"Surely not, Aunt Aelfrida," Antonia protested. "I believe they are a most hard-working sect and exceedingly charitable."

The Dowager Duchess sniffed. "Believing in hard work is all very well. Precisely what is to be encouraged among the lower orders. But Methodistical ideas on leveling the classes are most dangerous to the order of society. Social equality before God—I ask you. Would the Almighty have created the upper orders if he hadn't intended that society be well run?"

"And are you certain it is so well run, Aunt Aelfrida?" Danvers was shocked at his own words. Clearly his experiences of recent days had produced a profound effect on his thinking.

Fortunately, Aelfrida did not hear him, or chose to ignore his remark, as she continued. "It is entirely apparent. Unstable ideas produce unstable people. Look at Dove—"

"My dear duchess, perhaps we should let the trial tell its own story," Bramwell suggested.

"Nonsense. It's all common knowledge. The story's being cried on every street corner in York. Notoriously unbalanced. Expelled from school for bringing a gun into the classroom and threatening to shoot the master. Fortunately, one of his teachers confiscated the gun and he received a severe flogging from his father, whom he also threatened to shoot. And as if that weren't evidence enough he once set fire to a maid's cap. While she was wearing it."

"Aunt Aelfrida, how do you know all this?" Tonia asked.

"A quite wonderful broadsheet. It's all illustrated, including a drawing of Dove firing a pistol out the window after cornering his wife and threatening to shoot her if she moved. It's in my room. I'll be happy to show it to you after dinner, my dear."

"His poor wife," Tonia replied and turned her attention to the curried eggs and baked sweetbreads Humber offered her.

"Poor wife, indeed. That hardly expresses it. He poisoned her, after all. That is the point of all this," Aelfrida declared.

Bramwell cleared his throat. "Innocent until proven guilty, my dear duchess. The golden thread that runs like a river through English jurisprudence—innocent until proven guilty.

Dove is merely *accused* of poisoning his wife. My presence in the proceedings should be quite superfluous to requirement if we were not to uphold that principle as inviolate."

"Well spoken, Judge," Sir Gerald interposed. "And will you be able to enjoy a spot of angling while you're here? The River Nidd offers the finest fishing this side of Scotland."

The conversation shifted to the pleasures of compleat angling until the last succulent morsel of pineapple, freshly imported from the West Indies, had been enjoyed by all and the ladies withdrew. Sir Gerald passed the decanter of his best port to his guests. Judge Bramwell filled his glass, pushed back his chair, allowing more room for his not inconsiderable paunch and lit the fine Cuban cigar his host offered.

"I didn't like to discuss it in front of the ladies, of course, but I don't mind telling you we're in for an interesting week." Judge Bramwell said.

Sir Gerald took a sip of his port, "A lot of brouhaha being stirred up by the press, of course. Not just the broadsheets hawked by those running patterer fellows, but the legitimate press, too. Of course, I keep all that from Philomena—must do our duty to protect our womenfolk—although one hardly knows what to say to the dowager duchess." He shook his head. "But here they are, calling him the new Palmer."

"Sells papers, of course." Bramwell leaned back in his chair and took a long, thoughtful puff on his cigar. "Made a killing, Doctor Palmer did—if you'll pardon the expression. Collected a small fortune on life insurance from family members he apparently poisoned—although to be strictly correct his only conviction was of poisoning his friend with strychnia. Still, it was all for nothing—lost the whole thing gambling on horses."

Danvers joined the conversation, "From what I read of Dove's inquest, there doesn't seem to be much doubt about the accuracy of the coroner's jury finding cause of death as strychnia poisoning," he observed.

"What else could it have been?" Sir Gerald asked.

"Innocent until proven guilty, gentlemen." Bramwell stroked his bushy white side whiskers in thought. "There are conditions with similar symptoms—tetanus, hysteria, heart—but the medical testimony at the inquest was unusually competent. Great advance it was when the Medical Witness Act authorized coroners to pay for expert medical witnesses."

He took a long draw on his cigar and blew the smoke out slowly. "Confidentially, there's little enough doubt about the matter of strychnia. Question is the rest of the verdict 'willfully administered by her husband.'"

Danvers raised an eyebrow. "You question that Dove did it?"

"As I said, innocent until proven guilty, but I was really referring to the word 'willfully.'"

"What? You think it was an accident?" Sir Gerald asked.

"I'm interested in what constitutes 'will' under the law. Aelfrida was quite right about Dove's history of erratic behavior. A great deal came out before the coroner and I suspect we'll hear plenty more this week. Can someone with such aberrant history be judged to possess rational will?"

"But should a murderer be relieved of guilt if he's mad?" Danvers asked.

"Ah, significant question, indeed." Bramwell took another long, thoughtful puff on his cigar. "Well, we shall see what the defense makes of it all, but I'm certain we're in for a most interesting exhibition, gentlemen."

❧ 14 ❧

It seemed that all of York was astir for the opening of the Assize Court at two o'clock the next day. An alarming crush of vehicles jostled for position as the Wandseley carriage drew up in Minster Yard. It soon became clear that the cause of the jam was the arrival of the Sheriff's coach just ahead of them. Sir Gerald pointed out the dignitaries as they alighted from the closed black and gold carriage. First was the High Sheriff, in a tricorn hat, splendid robe and buckled shoes; the Sheriff's chaplain followed in a somber black robe; then the Under-sheriff. Last to alight as the liveried servant held the door, were Judge Bramwell and his fellow High Court judge from London.

Although they had arrived well ahead of time for the opening service, Antonia was concerned that there might not be seating left inside. Lady Wandseley assured her, however, that she need not worry. Since Sir Gerald, as a magistrate, was taking part in the procession, space had been reserved for his party near the front.

When the verger showed them to their seats, however, she discovered that 'near the front' was a relative term as the seats in the first quarter of the nave were reserved for the clergy, county officials and judges taking part in the procession. The rustle of silk gowns, hushed whispers and the scraping of feet on the tiled floor filled the air around them, but over all the full tones of the organ pealing a Handelian anthem emphasized the solemnity of the occasion.

At length the rustle settled as all the seats were full, and the organ pealed forth Handel's "Arrival of the Queen of Sheba." Then a commotion again filled the minster as all stood for the procession led by Crucifer, Taperers and the Cathedral Choir. The Diocesan Clergy preceded the clergy of the cathedral: The Residentiary Canons, the Dean's Verger, and Dean himself, all wearing colorful copes over black cassocks and white surplices. Behind him, in black knee breeches and white periwigs, the Deputy Registrar and the Registrar for the diocese. Then on to the civil dignitaries. The Sergeant at Mace led the Lord Mayor, aldermen, councilors, Sheriff and other officials of the city down the long aisle. Behind them followed the clerks, magistrates in their black robes with white bands at their necks, and the magnificently scarlet-robed, bewigged judges. Last of all, in solemn splendor, The Reverend Simon Jones, Doctor of Divinity, to whom had gone the prestigious honour of preaching the assize sermon.

When all were in place the congregation sang the opening hymn, Queen Victoria's favorite "Lead, Kindly Light," and at last they were allowed to settle into their seats with a profusion of rustling, coughing and shuffling of feet.

The Reverend Doctor Jones ascended the curving stairs to the high dark wood pulpit set against a massive stone pillar in the west aisle. After a lengthy acknowledgment of the many honoured guests, Jones announced his text, "'But thou shalt say unto them, This is a nation that obeyeth not the voice of the Lord their God, nor receiveth correction: truth is perished, and is cut off from their mouth.' Jeremiah 7:28."

All settled in to hear the preacher's words. More than once the words of an assize sermon had stirred lasting movements. No one wanted to be caught sleeping if this should be such an occasion.

"On public occasions, such as the present, the minds of Christians naturally revert to that portion of Holy Scripture, which exhibits to us the will of the Sovereign of the world in more immediate relation to the civil and national conduct of mankind...

"It behooves us, therefore, to avail ourselves of those national warnings, which fill the pages of Holy Scripture. Especially to those who would fain persuade themselves, that a nation, even a Christian nation, may do well enough, as such, without God, and without His Church.

"For those who think 'we will get rid of these disagreeable, unfashionable scruples, which throw us behind, as we think, in the race of worldly honour and profit' the scriptures of the Old Testament stand as perpetual warning to all who, having accepted God for their King, allow themselves to be weary of subjection to Him, and think they should be happier if they were freer, and more like the rest of the world..."

A hush blanketed the great cathedral as all seemed to lean forward as one in the grip of the preacher's words. The man spoke with a fire and an intensity that filled the space to the vaulted ceiling with the authority of an Old Testament prophet. Antonia shivered as she felt the importance of the words. "What is to be done to counteract this national apostasy, you ask. I call on all my hearers to make a new commitment. For each of our nation's anxious children, in his own place and station, to resign himself more thoroughly to his God and Saviour in those duties, public and private, of piety, purity, charity, justice."

Had this been a civil rather than a religious occasion, the speaker's words would have been met with a thunderous applause. As it was, mighty chords from the organ pealed forth in reply at the close of the deeply affecting sermon.

Antonia continued to feel held in the moment as the choir closed with a stirring rendition of "Zadok the Priest" and the dean closed in prayer. The entire company recessed out the great west doors of the Minster to a Bach prelude and fugue and the Assize Court for the northern Circuit was officially opened.

Uniformed and helmeted policemen, bearing long pikes, lined Precentor's Court as honour guard for the solemn procession proceeding on foot, a breeze billowing their robes as they made their way across the city toward Clifford's Tower high on the hill, to the classical, long stone building, it's front lined with Ionic columns and high, arched windows that housed the Assize Court.

Thinking more of resting Charles's leg than of her own comfort, Antonia suggested they follow the procession in the carriage with Philomena Wandseley and was pleased when Freddie accepted Lady Wandseley's invitation to join them. "Thank you, my lady. Just as far as Andrewgate, if you please. I must get on with my work."

"What did you think of the sermon?" Antonia asked as the carriage inched forward in the crush of traffic.

"Heartbreakingly fine," Freddie said with a shake of his head.

"What an odd expression."

"Ah, but all too true. 'Righteousness alone exalteth a nation.' Jones couldn't have chosen a finer theme for his job of admonishing the *civitas* on their duties. Yet how many of the listeners will put his words into practice? Power, prestige, money—that's what people care for. Who cares for righteousness?"

"Freddie, you're unaccustomedly morose."

"I couldn't help but think what a difference could be made if all the people in the hearing of that sermon today would truly heed it. It seemed much of it was similar to Keble's."

"John Keble, the poet?" Antonia often read from his popular book of poetry *The Christian Year* but she knew nothing of his preaching.

"Indeed, the same. It was his sermon, preached at the opening of the Oxford Assizes that launched the Oxford Movement. If only this sermon could produce such a stir. What if every such call to righteousness would cause all who hear it to devote himself entirely to the cause of righteousness? We could abate the triumph of disorder and irreligion we see all around us. We could—" He broke off suddenly.

"Forgive me, you're quite right, Tonia, I am much too morose."

The wheels of the carriage, thin strips of hard rubber over iron, clattered over the cobbles as Antonia considered. Was Freddie was being morose as she accused him? Or was he being realistic? Suddenly she had lost her appetite for more pomp. She turned to Danvers. "My love, would you mind terribly not going on to the court?"

He turned to her with concern. "Tonia, are you unwell? Do you have a headache?"

"No, not at all. I am quite well. But The Reverend Jones's call for action—the charity he urged. It was a powerful sermon, and I find I would rather be about it."

"You are quite right, my love. Bramwell mentioned that there are sixty-two cases on the assize calendar. Dove won't be called until tomorrow. I am quite ready for something more active after all that sitting, no matter how fine the sermon." He turned to his brother. "We shall join you in your good works, Freddie."

When they left the wider street and neared Bedern, though, Antonia wished she were wearing a less fine gown. No matter how much care she took in choosing where she stepped, her wide crinoline caused her silk skirt to brush against refuse piled against the buildings. She feared Isabella would be sore put to remove the stains from her hem.

Inside the asylum a few moments later, however, she had no fear for her skirt coming to harm from any dirt on the floors, but she wasn't certain how safe she was from splashes of soup as Hardy ladled with vigor.

She was tying the strings of a copious apron around her waist when a melodious young voice made her turn. "Lady Danvers, how charming to see you again."

"Victoria! Welcome back. Are you quite recovered?"

The girl smiled and her blue eyes twinkled. "No, I'm Cecilia. But don't worry, we're often confused. We used to play tricks on our music master if one of us was prepared for our lessons and the other not. He was terribly shortsighted and could never tell us apart."

"I am pleased to see you." Antonia gave the girl an impulsive hug. "And your sister, is she returned, too?"

The smile faded. "I fear not. She is some improved, but her physician isn't happy with her digestion yet. She remains at Harrogate with her maid, but I persuaded Father to let me return with him. He didn't want to miss the opening of the Assizes. He much admires Reverend Jones. Father often reads out his sermons to the servants when the household gathers for prayers."

"Were you there this morning?"

"No, but I'm certain I'll be hearing the sermon." She smiled. "Probably more than once."

Hardy and Danvers seemed to have the serving in the dining room well in hand, so Tonia asked Cecilia to help her prepare pap for Annie Rose. "Fetch a bread roll. We'll tear the soft insides into tiny crumbs and soak them well in sugar water. I'm so pleased to teach you this so you can do it for Betsy's baby when I'm not here."

Tonia fetched a small bowl to prepare the mixture in, and Cecilia returned in a moment with a warm roll and a small brown bottle."

"What's this?"

"Invigorating tonic. I thought it might be better than sugar water. Vicky said they often give it to women who need strengthening. She sometimes took it when she was having one of her weak spells."

Antonia pulled the cork from the top and sniffed. It smelled slightly sweet with a mildly astringent scent. Quite refreshing. Still, she had no idea what effect it might have on the digestion of a tiny infant. She put the cork back in the bottle. "Just plain water with a bit of sugar for now, I think. Perhaps when Annie Rose is a little stronger."

A few moments later Antonia led the way up the stairs. The familiar sounds of Iris's bitter complaining met them. "Can't someone shut 'er up? A body gets no peace around 'ere day or night." The only reply was another moan from the hugely pregnant Nan, which prompted another complaint from Iris.

Tonia bent over Betsy who was cuddling the tiny Annie Rose. "We've brought her some pap. My son's nurse says it will be just the thing."

Cecilia pulled a wobbly wooden chair over to the bed and sat. She produced the miniature spoon from a saltcellar she had found in the kitchen and held a few drops of the liquid bread to the rosebud mouth. "Just rub the spoon against her lips, Cece. When she opens her mouth, drop the pap in. Give her time to swallow that, then offer another."

Cecilia set about following Tonia's instructions, and Tonia turned to the bed at the end of the room. "How are you today, Millie?" The girl was ghostly pale, her eyes dark hollows; but were her cheeks perhaps just a little less drawn?

"Ever so much better, m'lady. Ah'm sure to be able to go 'ome in another day."

Tonia shook her head. "No, Millie. You must stay here until your baby comes. You both need care and nutrition."

"But the little 'uns. Ah worries about 'em in that place." She swallowed and looked at Antonia. "Don't take it amiss. Ah know tha means well. And Ah do thank'ee fer findin' 'em a place. But Ah'm that worried wot'll become of 'em."

"I'm sure there's nothing to worry about, Millie. The reverend took them there himself. And Lord Danvers. They saw it."

Her words did nothing to mollify her patient who continued to pluck at her blanket fretfully. "Millie, would you feel better if I looked in on them myself?"

The tension relaxed from Millie's face. She almost smiled. "Tha's ever so good, m'lady."

"That's settled, then. You rest. I shall bring you a first-hand report."

Downstairs Antonia smiled to find her tall, elegant husband wielding a mop under the eagle eye of Lady Billingston while Hardy carried buckets of water for the washing-up. "What a fine job you are doing, my love. When we return to Norwood Park you must oversee the house-maids. I'm certain you'll be able to teach Mrs. Pagnell new tricks."

"Not on your life. I'll not have our excellent housekeeper's routine disturbed for the world. She would give notice and without her and Bracken the entire establishment would collapse."

"Well, never mind. I've come to take you on an errand." She explained about visiting Millie's siblings.

Danvers leaned on his mop and looked at her. "You can't walk through Bedern in that dress." He turned. "Hardy!"

The sound of splashing ceased in the next room. "Yes, m'lord?"

"Procure us the services of a hackney cab, if you please. Although you may have to go all the way back to the Minster to find one unoccupied."

Hardy was lucky, however, and in a short time Charles was knocking on the door of the York Industrial Ragged School.

Antonia took a step backward and raised her hand to cover her mouth and nose when Louisa opened the door. "Wot do'st want?" The maid growled.

Danvers removed his top hat and sketched a bow. "We've come to call on the young lady we left in your care yesterday. If you would be so good as to fetch Miss Flossie."

"Wha'ssat?"

Danvers took a step forward. "Or if the young lady is engaged in her lessons you may bring Master Joey. Actually, we would be very happy to see all the children we brought in. Or perhaps you would prefer I enquire of Mr. Pimm myself?"

"'E's out."

"Then I suggest you find Flossie for us. I do not wish to comb this establishment myself."

"Wait 'ere." Louisa closed the door and left them on the pavement. A mangy dog slunk by. Tonia heard a scrabbling in the gutter she could only hope wasn't rats.

Sooner than Antonia might have guessed, however, the door opened again and Louisa thrust Flossie out on the street. "Don't know wot tha thinks this is? Fine ladies comin' visitin'. Ah suppose tha'll be wantin' me ter mash tha tea." The door slammed shut.

"Flossie, Millie is worried about you all, so we said we'd come see you. How are you?"

Flossie shrugged. "Ah's awreet."

"Are you certain? Are the others all right?"

Flossie nodded. "Sent Joe t' work in a market stall. 'E don't mind that, but Ah'm afeared they'll make Timmy sweep."

"Sweep? Crossings? But won't the larger boys push him away? He's so small." Antonia herself had often given a penny to a ragged lad who swept the street before her free of horse-droppings, but surely Tim was too small.

Flossie shook her head. "Nah, chimneys."

"What, Pimm plans to hire Tim out to a chimney sweep?"

"'E said as we hafta learn a trade. 'E's sendin' me an' Sukey an' Lettie to a farm when it's 'arvest time."

"But the girls are much too small. What about lessons? Have you begun those yet?"

"There was class. But Ah stayed with Mary Amelia. She's dreadful sick. And she's scared. So I 'eld her 'and until she slept. Like Ah seed thee do fer Millie that time."

"That was very kind of you, Flossie. But you mustn't miss your lessons. Learning to read is a fine thing."

Flossie nodded, looking at the ground.

"What about food?" Danvers asked. "Were you fed?"

Again Flossie nodded without looking up.

Tonia sighed. It was all exceedingly unsatisfactory, but she couldn't see anything more they could do at the moment.

✵ 15 ✵

D anvers looked up from his newspaper when Antonia entered the breakfast room the next morning. He started to fold it and tuck it out of sight, as was proper in the presence of a lady, although he suspected Tonia often read newspapers on the sly.

"Don't you dare hide that, my love," Antonia glared at his action. "You know I'm fairly bursting to hear the latest." She chose a kipper, eggs and baked tomatoes and mushrooms from the sideboard and sat in the chair Danvers pulled out for her.

Humber entered with a silver pot. "Coffee, m'lady?"

"Yes, please, Humber. The coffee here is excellent."

"Thank you, m'lady." He poured a steaming stream into her cup. "Mrs. Foss always grinds the berries herself. She says it's the only way she can be sure there's no chicory in it."

The butler had barely departed when Antonia leaned forward and demanded to hear all.

"William Dove's trial begins this morning. It is predicted to rival that of Doctor Palmer, the 'Prince of Poisoners.'"

Tonia shivered. "Horrid. 'The Monster of Poisoners'

would be more like it. It's quite bad enough to think of the adults he poisoned, but to think that he likely poisoned four of his own infants..."

Danvers nodded, even though this was far from an appropriate breakfast table conversation. "Yes, all for money to pay his gambling debts." Tonia's appellation of monster was quite appropriate, but he had no desire to dwell on the evil the heart of man was capable of conceiving. That was his brother's domain. Best to return to present events.

He glanced at the paper in front of him. "The High Sheriff has received ten times more applications for seats than the courtroom can hold."

"Then how fortunate for us that Sir Gerald has secured our tickets." The Dowager Duchess of Aethelbert swept into the room.

"Aunt Aelfrida, surely you don't mean to attend?"

The duchess chose only tea and toast for her breakfast. "You don't suppose I would miss all the excitement, do you?"

Danvers raised his eyebrows. "It promises to be a lengthy affair: thirty-three witnesses for the prosecution and twenty-four for the defense. The cost of the trial is projected to be not far off 2500 Pounds—the most expensive case this year after Palmer." He supplied a few more details, but there was no time to linger over a second cup of Mrs. Foss's excellent coffee. And, as he expected, his warnings did nothing to discourage the ladies in their desire to attend.

A fine mid-July morning with white clouds in a blue sky that promised warm sunshine greeted them a short time later as they drove up Tower Street. The closer they came to the Castle the thicker the posters were plastered announcing the forthcoming trial of the 'Leeds Poisoner' and the larger the crowds around the running patterers. Danvers noticed more than one making use of the Palmer murders, one of them hawking broadsheets divulging details of infants who died horribly of convulsions before their first birthdays. Danvers spoke more sharply than he meant to as he urged their driver to hurry on. Tonia had a strong constitution, but surely even she would have her limits. Many a fine lady would faint away at the mere suggestion of such horrors.

When they arrived at the Castle gates the swarm of onlookers was so great Danvers feared they might not get through. But just ahead of them a phalanx of policemen elbowed their way through the crowd, closely followed by a pack of some twenty reporters. "There, driver. Follow those rabbly journalists." Danvers feared Aunt Aelfrida would poke Sir Gerald's groom with her walking stick, but he obeyed her command quickly enough to avert the need for prodding.

Inside, the marble-floored, dark-paneled courtroom filled quickly, mostly with heavily-veiled, well-dressed ladies, many accompanied by their maids. When the clerk entered a few moments later and called, "All rise," the rustle of silk and the creak of whalebone gave further evidence of the preponderance of fashionable ladies among those who had come to view the horrid murderer.

Judge Bramwell entered and took his seat on a high, padded bench, perhaps twenty feet above the floor. The prosecutor and the counsel for the defense sat in leather-padded chairs at a long table almost directly under the judge's bench, piled with weighty, leather-bound legal tomes. The jurors sat in two rows with their backs to the high windows, facing the lawyers' table. The twelve men were each between the ages of 21 and 60, each with a guaranteed income from rents or lands, and lived in a house with not fewer than 15 windows—as the law prescribed.

To the juror's left was the elevated dock where the accused would stand. Public benches filled the room behind a railing separating them from the proceedings at the front. To the right, a gallery overhung the room where members of the press jostled one another to get the best view. Danvers was sure it wouldn't be long before the warmth and smell of so many bodies packed so closely would threaten to become overpowering.

In spite of the crowds, it was clear, though, that Judge Bramwell would run his courtroom on schedule. At precisely half past eight William Dove was led into the courtroom. The 35-year-old prisoner entered with a cocky step, his head up, exhibiting a tanned face and exuding an air of cheerful confidence and rude health.

When he was called to the bar Dove fairly tripped up the steps into the dock and struck a self-assured pose, left hand on his hip. "William Dove, you stand indicted for the willful murder of Harriet Dove, at Leeds, on the 1st of March last. Do you plead guilty or not guilty?"

Dove straightened slightly and replied in a firm voice, "Not guilty, my lord."

The jury was sworn in and Mr. Overend, counsel for the prosecution, rose to address the jury beginning with an admonition that they dismiss all rumors they might have heard and free their minds from prejudice and bias. He then moved swiftly to describe the case as one of the "most cold-blooded and cruel murders known in the history of crime.

"What we say on the part of the prosecution is, that the prisoner has committed murder by the use of a subtle poison known by the name of strychnia; that he used this poison on five or six different occasions; that he made five attempts on the life of his wife which were unsuccessful; and finally, that he made a sixth attempt, which ended in the death of Harriet Dove."

Overend then went into a lengthy explanation of how such poison was extracted from the *strychnos* bean. In the stuffy room Danvers's mind wandered. He recalled Mrs. Foss, the Wandseley cook explaining the careful extraction of the laurel water she used for flavoring delicate pastries, and how just such an extraction had caused the death of the maid Polly—by misadventure, the coroner had ruled. But the coroner had not ruled misadventure in the death of Harriet Dove, rather, willful murder.

After a lengthy recitation of Dove's mistreatment of his wife, promising the jury that they would soon hear witnesses testify to such facts, Overend again returned to the poison theme. "It will be proved to you that the facts of Palmer's case were brought to the knowledge of the prisoner at the bar, and that Dove had been assured that from evidence in that case, strychnia could not be discovered in the body."

Overend continued, outlining Harriet and William's often abusive married life: His addiction to liquor, even though he came from a very religious, highly respectable family; how he one time threw a chair at his wife's head; at another time, brandished a gun and threatened to blow her brains out; and again, menaced her with a rolling pin in his left hand and a carving knife in his right.

Then the prosecution chronicled her slow and painful death. Concluding that if, at the end of the trial the jury was convinced that Harriet died of poison administered by her husband, "You will be wanting in your duty to your country and your duty to God, if you do not find a verdict of guilty." After two hours and twenty-five minutes the learned counsel sat down.

The court adjourned for refreshment. Danvers stood and turned to offer his hand to Aelfrida to assist her to rise, but to his surprise the court clerk was already bowing over her hand. "His honour has asked that you join him in his chamber for luncheon, m'lady."

"How kind of him." She rose. "You will excuse me, nephew."

"Certainly, aunt." What a surprisingly gallant gesture for a man whom *The Times* had characterized as having 'no maudlin sentimentality.' He offered his arm to Antonia and they moved toward the door amidst a crowd anxious for fresh air and their midday meal.

"You are deep in thought, my love," Antonia said as they walked out onto the wide verandah in front of the courthouse. "What did you make of it?"

"Disturbing." He took in a deep breath of fresh air and signaled their carriage.

"Yes, it is disturbing," Tonia continued when she had settled her wide crinoline to the side to make room for her husband. "That poor woman, such a horrible way to die."

But Danvers was still distracted by his own thoughts. And the trouble was, he didn't even know what was disturbing him. "Yes, yes it is. But—forgive me, Antonia, my mind wasn't so much on Harriet Dove as it was on Polly and those other poor women who died at the Magdalen House."

"Yes, that's quite horrid, too, but I'm afraid I don't see the connection."

"No, nor do I. It was just all that Overend recounted about how Harriet had such repeated attacks, and Harriet herself telling her friends that 'whenever it is time to have any medicine, Mr. Dove is always ready by day or night to give it to me.'" He paused.

"What are you saying?" Antonia looked concerned.

"I don't know."

"Surely you don't suggest that the women at the Magdalen House died of strychnia? I don't recall any of the symptoms Freddie recounted to us being at all similar to Harriet Dove's. Of course, we've only heard Mr. Overend, not the actual testimony yet."

"Tonia, would you mind terribly if we didn't return for the afternoon session? When Overend was describing Dove's visit to the surgery of a medical practitioner in Leeds and the chest of shelves containing the various remedies and potions, including bottles of red antimony and strychnia, I couldn't help picturing just such a cabinet at the asylum."

"And you think there might be strychnia there?"

"I think it extremely unlikely, but I did wonder if a bottle could be mismarked or something administered incorrectly."

"I'm certain Lady Billingston is most careful. Still, there is the night nurse..." Tonia wrinkled her brow.

"Precisely. And various volunteers, many who come in when Lady Billingston isn't there."

They took their lunch in a public hostelry, eating cold game pie, pickle, and an assortment of vegetables in an atmosphere of friendly hubbub that was much at odds with the concern Danvers was feeling. For the first time he began to believe that there might be substance to Frederick's suspicions of foul play at the Magdalen House. And yet it made so little sense. Why would anyone bother? Overend had gone to considerable lengths to assign motive to Dove's action, describing his apparent desire to marry Mrs. Within, the attractive widow who lived next door. But surely, no one would have anything to gain from the death of the prostitutes and destitute women who came to the refuge. Their lives of hardship and poverty would surely see them in their graves in a short time without anyone having an evil hand in the matter.

The Magdalen House was as quiet as Charles had ever seen it. Freddie was directing two volunteers Danvers had not met before in cleaning up after the last of their soup-eaters had departed: the more fortunate of them had gone back to try their best at selling their meager wares on a street corner, or to the next shift in a factory or sweatshop; those not so lucky as to have employment returned to begging, thieving or escaping into a gin-soaked mist.

Carlotta Billingston wasn't there today. Tonia went upstairs to report to Millie on their visit to the school the previous day and, after greeting Freddie briefly, Danvers turned to explore the storeroom. As Freddie had mentioned when pointing it out earlier, there was precious little to store. A few well-worn, but clean sheets and blankets lay in tidy folds on one shelf. A cupboard next to it held several bags of dried peas, lentils and oats, no doubt procured from a local farmer by an insistent Lady Billingston. At least there was enough there to make several days'—perhaps a few weeks'—worth of porridge when donations of fresh vegetables failed to fill the stock pots.

On the opposite wall was what Danvers was looking for. Although now that he saw it he had no idea what he would make of it. A tall cabinet with glass doors covering its shelves contained bottles of liquid and boxes of herbs. Every item seemed to be clearly labeled and neatly arranged in alphabetical order: Antimonial Powder, Blister Compound, Calomel, Carbonate of Potash, Epsom Salts, Goulard's Extract, Aloes Pills, Nitre, Laudanum, Sal Ammoniac, Senna Leaves, Turner's Cerate...

Danvers shook his head. Surely all that was in order. Certainly nothing appeared to be hidden, but he had little idea of the properties of any of it. Three large bottles at the back were labeled Tonic. He recalled Tonia telling him about the tonic she declined to put in the pap for Annie Rose. Could there be something harmful in that? As there was in the tincture Polly swallowed, hoping for release from her troubles—

He pulled the cork from a bottle and sniffed just as he had at the bottle he found next to Polly. But the almost spicy scent of this brought no memory of the scent of the potion that had killed Polly.

He opened a drawer below the shelves and found further medical supplies: Adhesive Plaster, Isinglass Plaster, lint... He would have expected nothing less of the careful Lady Billingston.

"May I help you find something?"

The light female voice, coming a few feet behind his back, made him start so that he dropped the rolled bandage he was holding. It bounced across the floor like a ball and came to rest at Cecilia's feet. She stooped to pick it up and handed it back to him. "I'm sorry. I didn't mean to startle you."

"What a quiet footstep you have. I didn't hear you enter."

"You seemed deep in thought. Is there something particular you need? Oh," she started to turn to the door. "Is Millie in labor?"

"No, no, nothing like that. I was just, er—checking your supplies. I, uh—wanted to see how well equipped the asylum is."

She laughed. "Well, you can see that the answer is not very well. We do have Mrs. Beeton's complete list, though, you'll notice."

"Mrs. Beeton?"

"Yes, her *Book of Household Management*, Lady Billingston swears by it." She pulled a heavy, well-worn volume off a shelf. It fell open to a chapter near the back headed "The Doctor." "See, here is the author's list of everything necessary to carry out her instructions for home nursing. All volunteers at the asylum are instructed in it."

Danvers turned the pages: Bleeding from the nose, Bites and Stings, Fractures of Bones, Burns and Scalds... He looked at his hand, now wrapped only in a light bandage, and thought how recently he had had need to have recourse to such treatment. He turned a couple more pages and was about to hand the book back to Cecilia when his eye caught the section marked Poisons. A careful list, followed by their antidotes and remedies. Plenty of information available. Nothing, however, that seemed useful to answer his quandary.

His unformed suspicions were as vague as ever—too amorphous even to form a question. And yet the unease persisted.

※ 16 ※

"Thoroughly riveting. Wouldn't miss it for the world." Antonia had not had a chance to hear the Dowager Duchess's opinions on yesterday's trial until they were again in the carriage, heading across York toward the Castle, although this morning they travelled in a closed carriage as the sky was dark and threatened rain.

"Do you believe him guilty, aunt?"

"Certainly. No doubt of it at all. And the gel knew it, too —she saw it coming."

"His wife?"

"Assuredly. That maid, Elizabeth Fisher, she testified that Harriet Dove said to her, 'Elizabeth if I should die, it is my wish that you should tell my friends to have my body examined.' And Dove showed Fisher the strychnia—used it to kill a rat and a cat."

Tonia shook her head, the wide brim of her bonnet brushing the edge of the carriage seat. "But why did Harriet stay with him if she thought her life in danger?"

Aelfrida scoffed. "She was as unstable as he was. I've read

all about how she romped with him and entered into his childish games."

"*Read*, Aunt Aelfrida? Do you mean to tell me you are still indulging in broadsheet tittle-tattle?" Danvers raised an eyebrow.

"Certainly not. Only those my maid leaves lying about. It's my duty to inspect her reading."

Today the courtroom seemed even more tightly packed than the day before, perhaps because more tickets were held by women and their wide crinolines and veiled bonnets took up more space. Dove's childhood nurse Mary Wood was the first witness to be sworn in. Mary was a small, upright woman, her gray hair tucked tightly behind the brim of a plain black bonnet. Tonia felt this was just such a nurse as a strict Methodist household like the Doves would choose, a nurse who would tolerate no nonsense in her young charges.

After Mary Wood's initial statement detailing her fifteen years of service in the Dove household, beginning when the prisoner was five years old, Mr. Bliss, Dove's defense counsel, asked, "Did you form an opinion as to the state of his mind?"

Overend, the prosecutor, was instantly on his feet, objecting to the question.

Judge Bramwell consulted a legal volume presented to him by the counsel. Antonia could feel the electricity in the air as the judge considered. Patterers and newspapers had primed the public on this issue, which seemed sure to arise. This was a scientific question which could be put to a medical man. But could it be asked of an unscientific person like Mary Wood? The outcome of the trial, and indeed, of the future of English law could hang on this ruling.

At last Bramwell closed the volume and cleared his throat. "The question may not be put."

A discontented murmur swept through the room. Antonia felt her own disappointment. She wanted to know the answer to the question.

Mr. Bliss was on his feet. "My lord, this question is not a scientific one. I merely asked the witness for the impression produced upon her mind by facts and circumstances within her own knowledge."

Another counselor interjected that if the witness were debarred from answering it would exclude all evidence of the state of the prisoner's mind from his earliest years—evidence which might prove the prisoner insane from birth. "And," he added, "In the United States of America such questions are allowed."

Whalebones creaked as hearers leaned forward, awaiting Bramwell's ruling.

"Mr. Bliss, you may put the question in the form in which you desire it to be answered."

Bliss turned to the witness in her high, pulpit-like box. "From your observation of the prisoner's conduct, disposition and behavior during the fifteen years you were in the family, did the prisoner appear to you to be of sane mind?"

The room held its breath. "I never thought the prisoner was right in his mind." Mary Wood's tone of voice, set of head and firmness of mouth all spoke of the sureness of her opinion.

She went on to detail events that led her to that opinion. "I once saw a great light in his bedroom one night. He refused to let me in. Next morning, I found that he had thrown strong spirit on the curtain and set it on fire, then thrown water on it to put it out.

"I have seen him chase his sisters with a red-hot poker and known him to hang a cat by the tail out of the bedroom window.

"Once he had from an accident a great gash on his arm

which was almost healed. He took a sharp-pointed knife and cut it open again, saying it had healed false. He liked to prick himself with the knife and write his name in his own blood.

"The family was very pious and religious and great pains were taken to instruct the prisoner properly, but he could not be readily taught his religious lessons.

"He took a great deal of looking after."

Throughout the questioning of the next witnesses Antonia's mind was on Mary Wood's testimony. She looked at the prisoner standing in the dock. He appeared to be every bit as cool and unbothered as he had the day before. Was this a naughty, rebellious boy grown into an evil man? Or was he, as the defense seemed to be implying, a human being to be pitied because he had been born without the capacity for rational thought? Or was it possible Dove's calm, confident demeanor was truly the result of knowing himself to be innocent?

The next great stir occurred when the clerk announced, "Call Henry Harrison to the bar."

Again, the patterers had primed the audience. Antonia herself recognized the name as one she had heard proclaimed on more than one street corner. Stories of the Witch-man had sold many broadsheets, recounting the escapades of the fifty-year-old astrologer, dentist and water-caster. When his career as water-caster, or urine scryer, had floundered—apparently he had been unable to detect the cause of his patients' illnesses by observing the color and consistency of their urine —he pursued clients as a magician.

Harrison testified that Dove had consulted him first for magical help in retaking the land he had once farmed but whose lease he had lost due to mismanagement. Harrison told the court he had secreted coppers in the farm's cardinal points for his client and afterwards Dove had introduced him to Harriet and invited him to stay for dinner. In the course of the evening Harrison had observed that Harriet looked unwell. He prescribed a mixture of gentian, juniper berries, valerian and aniseed extract.

Dove later sought Harrison for an astrology reading but the wizard testified he never completed Dove's nativity chart because of the state of his client's mind: "He was easily made drunk and was always talking of being haunted by devils and spirits accompanied by thunder and lightning. He told me he had sold his soul to the devil, but he thought I had greater power over the devil than he and that I could send the devil to frighten his wife from her own bed to go to sleep with him.

"He said there were spirits in the house and repeatedly spoke about having sold his soul to the devil."

Tonia returned to her earlier thoughts. Was Dove insane or evil? The idea of his innocence seemed less likely as Harrison recounted a conversation he had had with the prisoner regarding the Palmer case. "Dove asked if I could get or make him some strychnia? I said, 'No.' He said, 'Why not? If you won't, I will get some somewhere else.'

"On Thursday, March 6th, I was sent for by the prisoner who gave me a funeral card of his wife, and said there was to be an inquest. I said, 'What for?' He said, 'Can they detect a grain or grain and a half of strychnia?' I said, 'Why, have you given her some?' He said, 'No, but I got some and gave it to a cat. The cat is in the midden. My wife might have got some.'

"I said, 'Go back, if you are innocent. What need have you to be frightened: They will not take you.'"

The trial continued with Harriet's mother reading out several very polite, considerate letters her son-in-law had written to her, including the last one from his prison cell in York Castle. Then she recounted, with heart-wrenching hindsight, Tonia felt, of taking Harriet and William to a lawyer to have papers of separation drawn up, but the couple became friendly again and they all returned home together.

The final witness that morning was Harriet's sister Mrs. Risdon who recounted confronting the prisoner after her sister's death. "I said he had caused her death because by his conduct he caused her to have hysterica. He said she did not die from hysterics. I thought she had died from hysterica. I know she was subject to hysterics. She had hysterics before her marriage. The symptoms were like spasms in the stomach. She had twitches, her arms moving sharply and suddenly."

The discussion of symptoms continued. In reply to a question from Judge Bramwell the witness continued: "There was a sound of wind rattling in her stomach; her hands were stiff, and her arms twitched..."

Gripping as the morning's proceedings had been, Tonia felt she had had all she could bear for one day. The newspapers had informed them that morning that expert medical evidence would take up the afternoon. Tonia was certain she could be of more use putting what little medical knowledge she had to practical use at the Magdalen asylum. Millie, although touchingly pleased to see her yesterday, had seemed very dispirited, and tiny Annie Rose had taken a few spoonfuls of her pap, but then fell back to sleep. Perhaps today would be better.

Danvers was quite willing to accompany his wife to the Magdalen House, so once again they left the Dowager Duchess to her own devices. This time they arrived just as the soup was being served. Antonia couldn't help smiling at the sight of her husband removing his top hat and wielding, somewhat stiffly, a large wooden ladle pouring cabbage soup into the bowls held out to him by the line of unwashed humanity shuffling past.

Tonia likewise removed her bonnet, but turned her steps

to mount the creaking stairs. She went first to Millie's bed, hoping to find her patient improved. Millie was dozing. Even in her sleep, however, she moved restlessly, tangling the sheets. The pale light from the grey sky coming through the small window fell across Millie's face, making her appear an unnatural ashen hue. Tonia did what she could to straighten the sheet over the girl's distended abdomen, then, as an afterthought, took a small vial from her reticule and sprinkled a few drops of lavender-water on her pillow, hoping it would soothe her.

How Millie was able to sleep was a mystery to Tonia since Nan was moaning as if she were in labour and Iris continued her usual stream of complaints. Cecilia sat on a low stool by Betsy's bed, holding minuscule spoonfuls of pap to Annie Rose's tiny pink mouth while Betsy looked on beaming. "She's growed a'ready. Don't tha think?"

Tonia agreed. A few days ago she had despaired over the child's life, but now she could see definite signs of hope. And yet, hope for what? What future could they offer this infant whose life they had fought to save?

"Did you attend the trial this morning?" Cece asked after they had exhausted the possibilities of cooing over their infant charge.

Tonia agreed that she had, indeed, and that the crush was even greater than the day before. "Many were being turned away when we arrived." She smiled. "All of them ladies."

"Was it a great sensation? Who gave testimony today?"

Antonia considered. Murder and madness were not topics for the sickroom. Cheerfulness, light and fresh air were Miss Nightingale's prescription. There had been little enough of that in the morning's proceedings.

"Ow, can't tha shut 'er up, t' miserable cow?" Iris picked up a bottle that had been left by her bed and chucked it at

Nan. "Off 'er 'ead she is. Can't nobody get any peace around 'ere."

Antonia decided an account of the courtroom might at least take their minds off their present misery. Or, as the saying went, 'misery loves company.' She supposed she could provide company. She summarized the question of whether the accused was mad or bad by telling some of the childhood misdemeanors Mary Wood had recounted. Iris thought hanging the cat out the window by its tail amusing. She actually came the closest Antonia had ever seen to smiling.

Then she moved on to tell of the mistreatment Harriet Dove had received at her husband's hand. "And the real tragedy is that her mother arranged a separation for her, but Harriet chose to go back to her husband," she concluded.

"An' why not?" Iris's high-pitched voice demanded. "Wot's a few pranks? Right silly cow she'd be to leave a comfort'ble 'ouse because 'er man waved a knife around."

Tonia was shocked into silence.

"Didn't give 'er no broken bones, did 'e? Not even so much as a black eye. Coddled, that's wot she were. 'E was in 'is drink. Wot'd she expect?"

Tonia was too shocked to point out that the man had apparently administered a deadly poison to his wife. That was hardly a simple prank. Nothing could have given her a starker picture of what Iris's life must be like than her attitude to Harriet Dove's situation.

After a moment Antonia simply continued as if Iris hadn't spoken. "The last witness was some sort of conjurer or confidence man named Henry Harrison."

"Oh," Cecilia spoke so suddenly she startled Annie Rose who emitted a little cry. "Shhh, little one. Sorry. There now, that's all right," she soothed the infant. When Annie was settled she continued. "Harrison? The witch-man?"

"Yes, it seems Dove had consulted him on several occasions. What do you know of him?"

"I'm not sure, but Madge Broadbent, one of the prisoners I visit—You know my regular charity work is prison visiting?"

Tonia nodded. Cece had taken so well to the asylum work filling in for her sister, that Tonia had forgotten this wasn't her usual charity service.

"She was an abortionist, but Madge is very repentant and determined to live a Christian life—for the little time she has left—one of our most successful cases—truly reformed. You should hear her sing hymns when we visit her."

"But Harrison, what does she have to do with him?" Tonia prompted.

"I don't know, but I'm certain she mentioned his name."

The conversation might have gone on, but just then Millie wakened and Tonia went to her side. "How are you today? Did you have a good nap?" She tried to sound cheerful in spite of her dismay at the girl's drawn look.

"Oh, yes, lovely thank you." Millie's smile seemed forced, and her voice was weak.

"Could you eat something? I'm afraid it smells like cabbage soup today, but if you could manage a little..."

Tonia felt guilty when Millie's eyes lit up at the mention of cabbage soup. She had to remember that cabbage probably constituted a treat for the girl who had scrabbled so hard to feed her young brothers and sisters. "I'll get you some." She fled before she could be engulfed by pity and hopelessness. She could never feed all the hungry in the slums of York, but she could feed those in front of her.

She returned a few minutes later with a bowl of steaming, if smelly, soup and the largest of the fresh bread rolls. She helped Millie to sit up, propping a pillow between her thin back and the iron bedrail and sat, trying to think of cheerful, encouraging things to say to the girl as she ate. "And you mustn't worry about Joey and Floss and the little ones. The school seemed a bit disorganized, but I'm sure Mr. Pimm is assiduous about teaching the children a trade. After all, he's hired by the city corporation, and paid well for it." She spoke as much to reassure herself as to comfort Millie. The smell of the cabbage soup reminded her of the stale stench that had threatened to nauseate her when they visited the industrial school, but she wouldn't bother Millie about that. Surely it was nothing a good airing-out couldn't fix. Perhaps the orphans needed stricter supervision in the matter of emptying their chamber pots. "And lord Danvers and I will visit them again in a day or two."

When Millie laid her spoon aside Tonia was happy to see her bowl empty, but disappointed that her cheeks held no more color. Millie shook her head when Tonia offered to bring her more food. "I would like to see you looking more vigorous, Millie. You'll be giving birth any day now, and that's extremely hard work. We really do need to get your energy up."

Tonia took the empty bowl to the kitchen where, in the absence of female volunteers, Danvers, Freddie and Hardy were doing the washing-up. Tonia smiled and turned toward the hall where she noticed the door to the supply room was open. Carlotta Billingston was working at a small table, pouring a dark liquid into brown glass bottles with a funnel.

"Good day, Carlotta."

Carlotta started so she spilled a quantity of the liquid onto the table. "Oh, Antonia. I wasn't aware you were here."

"No, I've been upstairs with Millie. I'm not at all happy about her. I don't think she has the strength for childbirth."

Carlotta smiled, "Well, that's easily enough remedied. I've been trying to get her to take my restorative tonic. But the silly girl refuses. You'd think I was trying to poison her. Perhaps if you offer it to her." She held out a bottle.

"What is it?" Tonia dipped her finger in the small puddle that had spilled on the table and noted the aromatic, slightly astringent smell. She licked her finger and made a face at the bitter taste. Little wonder Millie didn't want to take it. "What is it?"

"*Laurus nobilis*, it's an excellent appetite stimulant. We use it to treat colic, gas and indigestion."

"Oh, yes," Antonia recalled, "your cook explained its restorative properties to me."

"It's also useful externally as a rub on rheumatism, sprains and bruises. But then you are undoubtedly aware of that."

Tonia frowned, wondering why she should be.

"I observed your husband limping. I gave a bottle to Hardy with instructions to rub it on his lordship's leg. I've noted that he uses his stick very little since then." Carlotta looked satisfied and held a bottle out to Tonia.

"Excellent. I'll try to make Millie see sense."

Millie, however, was obdurate.

"Don't be silly," Toni coaxed. "I know it tastes awful, but you want to do what's best for your baby."

Antonia's patient set her lips.

Antonia started to argue when she was distracted by a clatter on the other side of the room. "Wot's tha playin' at now? Ah've not slept a wink in twen'y-four an' just when Ah nods off—" Iris's whining voice called Tonia's attention to the bed where a spasm from Nan had knocked a bottle onto the floor.

Tonia crossed the room to retrieve it. "Here now, no harm done." She picked up the bottle, then realized the cork had come out and its contents spilled onto the floor. She sighed, now she would have to go downstairs and find a mop. First, though, she would straighten Nan's covers. Fortunately, the disturbance hadn't wakened her.

The woman's arm hung awkwardly off the side of the bed,

perhaps she had gone to sleep with the bottle in her hand, then jerked in response to a dream. Tonia reached to place Nan's arm in a more comfortable position, then drew back.

With a gasp she turned and fled down the stairs.

Danvers met her at the bottom and she all but fell into his arms. "It's Nan. She's dead."

❧ 17 ❧

The next morning Frederick sat in the Wandseley withdrawing room with his head in his hands. "Oh, yes, it will be ruled a natural death—what could be more 'natural' than for an ill, malnourished, expectant woman to die in Bedern? It happens every day. Many times a day. But that's what we're meant to prevent. We're supposed to be there to give life and hope. I want to bring goodness into the world, not provide a place to see women and children out of it and into a pauper's grave."

He jumped to his feet and began pacing the room making a track in the Aubusson carpet as he circled the central table tastefully draped with a silk-fringed shawl. Their present genteel surroundings, so at odds with the environs of the Magdalen House and the tales of madness and violence they had been hearing of in court in recent days, made a jumble of contrasting pictures in Danvers's mind and prevented him from offering any coherent advice or comfort to his brother. What a failure they had all been.

Certainly he had failed to achieve any of the purposes for which they had come to York. The time had been anything but a peaceful respite for himself and Antonia. His injured leg was being blessedly slow to heal and still ached like fury every night. And they had made no progress toward helping Frederick understand what was going on at his asylum. Indeed, if one included Polly's death, there had been three additional deaths since their arrival.

The thought of returning to Norwood Park to oversee the rebuilding presented a most appealing picture. But, little help though he had been, he could hardly abandon Frederick at this crushing moment.

"What's to become of the Magdalen House?" Freddie continued his lament. "I don't know how many more disasters we can withstand. I was so sure about the rightness of this work. I know it's the ministry I'm called to. And yet... Word of every death spreads like wildfire through Bedern and beyond. We're an object of gossip as it is. And now women are afraid to come to us. And we're losing what little support we have from our patrons. One volunteer resigned just this morning and two patrons removed their names from our subscription list."

Danvers was still searching about for some encouragement to offer that wouldn't sound patronizing when the door opened and the Dowager Duchess entered, tapping her walking stick for attention. Freddie stopped pacing and straightened his stooped shoulders. Danvers sprang to his feet.

"Charles, I'm not accustomed to being kept waiting. Nor is it good manners to keep Sir Gerald's coachman hanging about. I don't know what you two are nattering on about in here, but I'm certain it's nothing that can't be continued in the carriage." She gave them both a closer look through her lorgnette. "Or perhaps left unsaid. Fretting over that female are you?"

Neither man answered.

"Yes, I see you are. Now you listen to me, Frederick William Leighton, you did your best. You gave the gel a clean, soft bed. How many of her likes ever have that? And if she paid any attention to the prayers and Bible reading you offer before every meal in that place, we can hope she has gone to a better place than she ever knew here. What more can you ask?" She turned and swept from the room, her crinoline making a soft swishing across the carpet, her orders for them to follow her unspoken.

Freddie's face was a study in amazement. "Best close your mouth, brother," Danvers said as he turned toward the door, suppressing a smile.

Danvers ordered the coachman to drop Freddie at the asylum before driving on up Castle Hill. It was as well Aunt Aelfrida had chivvied them to action, for the courtroom was packed beyond capacity a full hour before the trial was to begin. Undoubtedly the fact that today the prisoner's counsel was to begin his defense had roused public curiosity to even greater pitch.

Jury, counsel, and witnesses filed in. Judge Bramwell took his seat on the elevated bench. The rustle of silk, slithering of feet and soft coughing that filled the room began to settle down, but then increased when William Dove was once again escorted to the dock, exhibiting the good spirits he had maintained throughout the trial.

Bliss, the learned defense counsel rose and turned directly to the jury. "Gentlemen of the Jury, the case for the prosecution is over, after continuing two long days, during which you have seen the power of the whole community arrayed against a man least able to defend himself, and during which nothing has been spared that eloquence, and skill, and ability, and learning, and industry, and science could supply to place him beyond hope or mercy—almost beyond all claim to your pity.

"I regret that even we could not approach this hall of

justice without seeing placarded upon the walls, 'Trial of Dove, the Leeds Poisoner.' But now I ask you to question whether there has been a murder at all, and I pray you to look into the state of the facts. I ask you to approach this inquiry with a clear judgment and a mind free from prejudice.

"It is all a question of reason. I give you, a family—the one an invalid, who had long suffered from hysteria and indigestion—the other an unwise and a weak man occasionally drunk. As you heard, poison was brought into that house to poison cats and mice. Is this not a prescription for accident? Does not all reason cry out that in these circumstances a mishap is almost certain to occur? The poison might be spilt in some way. It is a light substance, could it not easily blow into the tapioca? Could not a visitor look into the snuffbox on the mantle, in which the prisoner has told us he kept the substance, and easily let some escape? It was put on meat and cheese for the offending vermin. Could it not have gotten into human food as well by mischance?

"Does anybody say he saw that man administer poison to his wife? None. All the evidence is circumstantial."

Danvers was impressed with the skill of the defense counsel. Yesterday everyone had left court believing the outcome of the trial to be a foregone conclusion—indeed, everyone had come in the first day believing that. But in the space of less than an hour Bliss had succeeded in making his hearers look at the evidence differently, to consider alternatives.

He now continued by developing the line that Harriet had not died from poison at all, but rather from a violent attack of frenzied panic "After all, the lady had been subject to hysteria and was under treatment for hysteria at the time. Her medical man Mr. Morley saw her daily and another was with her during two of the attacks. They heard their patient's description of the attacks, and they came to the conclusion that the attacks were hysterical. It was only after hearing the evidence in this case that they changed their opinion.

"Mrs. Dove herself, who knew her symptoms best, judged that she was suffering hysteria, as she had so many times throughout her life. Indeed, you have heard, and you will hear again, family members testify to the fact that Harriet Dove was subject to hysteric fits, that they commenced upon the loss of a brother in her early childhood and that she was subject to them ever afterwards. Having heard the circumstances of the case, members of the family are convinced that her death resulted during an hysteric fit.

"But let us suppose the unfortunate Mrs. Dove did, indeed die of poisoning. And let us suppose it to have been administered by the prisoner as he stands accused before you today. Let us consider the matter of his responsibility in the matter. Let us begin with the many references you have heard to the case of William Palmer, which was brought up many times by the prisoner himself. There was nothing in Palmer's case to encourage Dove to use strychnia to poison his wife; but on the contrary, there was everything in it to warn him against it. Palmer's case filled everybody's mind with horror and detestation. Palmer's case showed that strychnia poisoning could be proved. Palmer was executed.

"There was nothing, therefore, to encourage the use of strychnia. Nothing, that is, to encourage a sound mind. But, if the accused is insane, Palmer's case was the very thing to suggest strychnia, because, in insanity, the impulse to imitation is irresistible.

"So let us examine this obscure and mysterious disease—insanity. Indeed, as cases of moral madness have become more frequently recognized, an act of parliament was passed to provide that in those cases where the prisoner was acquitted on the ground of insanity, he should be confined so long as he was dangerous. It is now recognized that the acting under any delusion caused by insanity is sufficient to excuse him from the commission of a crime perpetrated under that delusion.

"So let me remind you of the testimony we have heard which gives evidence of such disease of the mind and defect of understanding in the case of the prisoner that shows he had not the power of distinguishing between right and wrong. You have heard of how he used to fire arms off without an object, how he rode about furiously on a horse and into a pond when the horse was covered with foam, how he chained a bulldog to the oven, threw water on a maidservant and burnt her cap—whilst she was wearing it. He also gave strange orders about his farm: he planted apple trees one day, and cut them down the next; he went strolling about the fields crying and threatened to blow up his farm and set it on fire; and when his neighbor harvested ripened corn, the prisoner cut his own while still green.

"Likewise you will recall testimony of how, at another time, he packed up his stockings saying he was going to enlist for a soldier, then was found in the shed covered with hay; how he put a pistol to his own mouth and threatened to shoot himself; and how he claimed to have grown black potatoes worth 50,000 pounds."

Bliss paused and turned to the counsel's table, shuffled through some papers, drew one out, and turned to the jury with a flourish. "But before we hear the evidence of more witnesses to substantiate these arguments I have placed before you for your consideration, let me share one last piece of irrefutable evidence of the prisoner's insanity. Irrefutable, because it is in his own handwriting. Nay, in his own blood." A gasp of horror filled the courtroom as Bliss held the paper out at arm's length for the jury to see.

"Gentlemen, I hold before you a letter written not many yards from you, in a cell at York Castle and found sewed up in the prisoner's clothing." Bliss paused for full effect, then pronounced in somber tones, "A letter to the devil."

The courtroom exploded in an outcry of astonishment and horror. One lady in the back screamed and fainted. She had to be helped from the courtroom by an usher. It was several minutes before Bramwell could be heard above the uproar. "Silence! I will have order in my courtroom or I will direct the bailiff to clear the court."

Eventually the clamor subsided and Bliss could continue. He adjusted his silver-rimmed spectacles, straightened the paper and cleared his throat. "Dear Devil,"

The intake of breath in the courtroom was so sharp, and the murmur in the gallery so loud that Bliss was again obliged to wait for quiet while Bramwell glared with a particularly hard eye at the journalists leaning over the gallery.

Bliss cleared his throat again. "Dear Devil," he repeated for emphasis, "If you will get me clear at the assizes, and let me have the enjoyment of life, health, wealth, tobacco, beer, more food and better, my wishes granted, and live till I am sixty, come to me and tell me. I will remain your faithful servant. William Dove."

Danvers waited for the inevitable outcry from the hearers of such a travesty, but instead there was only a long release of breath as if an expression of great sadness. Or fear.

Bliss paused, removed his spectacles, then continued. "It is awful to contemplate that a man could write such a letter. It is sad to think that humanity should be subjected to such baseness as this. It is enough to make us weep for our infirmities, though others may laugh. I confess I feel more disposed to go and pray my Maker to deliver us from such a one as this.

"I now leave the case in your hands. Gentlemen, it is a dreadful task for you to perform. If you think, after this, it would be edifying to society—if you think it will tend to the repression of crime; if you think that the law requires that a man who believes he has sold his soul to the devil—who, under this dreadful, this impious, this insane delusion—should be hanged at York Castle for an example, I ask you why? As an example to whom? To the insane? Alas! They are never governed by rational example.

"You are not called here to avenge anything, you are not called here in the vain expectation that the hanging of one person can make amends for the poisoning of another. You are called here simply to inquire whether you believe a man, of whose mind you have had this unhappy picture, and of whose progress through life you will have my sad history confirmed, is a man who is to be held accountable for his actions and executed on the scaffold, or whether he is a man to be confined as a lunatic as the law in such cases provides." The defense had spoken for five hours.

Bliss sat down. And Danvers stood. He simply must stretch his legs. He had no doubt of the testimony that would follow. It would confirm all that Bliss had said it would. And all that Overend had already asserted. But Danvers did not wish to hear more of this sad, confused case.

He was outside the courthouse before he realized Tonia was beside him. "Forgive me for not taking proper leave of you, my dear. I felt I could sit there no longer."

"Nor I, my love. If you hadn't risen I should have anyway. Aunt Aelfrida was so rapt she merely waved me away." Tonia held her hands out to the gentle mist, too light to be properly called rain. "Oh, I wish it were heavier. I feel as if I could use a good washing after that. Those poor, mad people. Surely Harriet was as weak-minded, if not as vicious, as her husband. What a tragedy for all concerned."

Her speech had taken them across the flagged verandah. Danvers offered his arm to his wife and descended the first step. Whether he misstepped or whether he was cramped from such a long period of enforced sitting, or whether the flags were uneven he didn't know, but whatever the cause he stumbled heavily and only saved himself from a fall by grabbing the iron railing.

"Oh, my love, are you hurt?" Tonia grasped his arm.

"It's this blasted leg. Surely it should be healed by now."

Tonia's voice was only slightly firmer than if she had been addressing their son. "No, my love, it is not the injury. It is your own impatience. That and your insistence on overdoing. *Rest* your doctor said. And how much ease have you given it? You threw your stick away days ago. Prematurely, obviously." She raised her hand to signal a waiting hackney cab. "I know just the remedy. Only yesterday Carlotta was telling me how effective her tonic is for sprains, bruises and all such like."

He started to protest, but she held up a hand as they walked slowly toward the cab, Tonia holding his arm with both hands. "You needn't deny it. She told me she had given Hardy a bottle for you, but I'm confident you have refused its application."

"Nightly. And forcefully. And I see no reason to change my mind now." But he did not shake off Tonia's support in spite of the impulse of his pride to do so.

And once at the Magdalen House he did submit to sitting in the privacy of Lady Billingston's office and allowing Antonia to administer the liniment rub. Although he absolutely refused to admit that its astringent warmth, as well as her caressing fingers, felt very nice, indeed.

Tonia had just completed her ministrations when there was a light knock at the door. "Come," Danvers barked.

When he saw the stricken look on Cecilia's face Danvers was sorry that his voice had sounded so harsh. He started to ask if he could be of assistance to her, but Tonia was quicker to speak. "Cece. What is wrong?" Her hand flew to her mouth. "Oh, not another—" She looked toward the upstairs nursing room. "Not Annie Rose?"

"No, no. She's fine. I'm sorry to have frightened you, but I'm so worried." She held out a sheet of creamy vellum paper inscribed with a flowing, feminine hand. "It is from Victoria. She is no better and she is terribly bored at Harrogate with only her maid for companion. Selina is a bit of a termagant. She has taken care of us since we were little—our mother died at our birth—but she can be overprotective. And our father is in London on business affairs..." She caught her breath in a little hiccough.

Antonia moved to put her arm around the girl. "How very fortunate. Lord Danvers and I were just discussing how very pleasant it would be to go to Harrogate."

"We were?" Danvers asked almost under his breath.

Tonia ignored him. "What a shame it would be if we were to spend so much time in your lovely Yorkshire and see no more of the county." She turned to her husband. "I know you're longing to get out of the city, Charles. Shall we take the aerostat?"

Danvers sat back in his chair, grinning. Long experience had taught him there was no point in trying to rein Tonia in once she had the bit between her teeth. He waved his hand in acquiescence.

"Oh, thank you, thank you! You are so kind." Cecilia gave Tonia an impulsive hug and dashed from the room. They heard her light step tripping up the stairs to see to her charges.

"Just discussing it, were we?" Danvers asked with a raised eyebrow.

"Well, we would have been quite at that precise moment if Cece hadn't interrupted. I was just going to suggest that we go to Harrogate for you to take the waters."

Danvers jerked upright. "Me? What fustian! How many times must I tell you? I am not an invalid."

She pushed him gently back in the chair. "Oh, but my

love, just think how delightful the Turkish baths will feel! It is exactly what your medical man would advise for you."

Danvers submitted with an amused grace. "Well, it's obviously what my wife would advise."

"Whatever have you done for Cece?" Freddie entered the office. "I haven't seen her so happy for days. I think she's been missing Victoria quite dreadfully."

Tonia quickly filled her brother-in-law in on their plans. "And you must go with us, Frederick. You work far too hard."

He started to protest. But she continued. "How long has it been since you've taken a break?" He was silent. "Have you had one since taking up your living?"

"Well—there's always so much to do..."

"Precisely why you need to remain refreshed so you can give your best to your parish."

The men exchanged a look that said that submitting would be much easier than arguing. Besides, they would undoubtedly lose in the end.

So it was agreed that they would leave the last day of William Dove's trial to the capable scrutiny of the Dowager Duchess and they would escort Cecilia to Harrogate. Frederick would, of course, have to return Saturday evening to conduct Sunday services at Saint Alphege's, but the others would remain longer. In the end, Freddie agreed to escort Isabella on the train with their bags, arriving ahead of the ballooning party so he could arrange transport to take them from the open countryside outside Harrogate into the city. Hardy would go in the balloon and then see that it was ready for Frederick's return that evening.

"There, that's most satisfactory." Tonia gave Danvers a brilliant smile and bent to plant a kiss on his forehead. "Just rest here, Charles. I'll run upstairs and see how Millie is progressing."

Antonia's elation over the happy prospect of a visit to

Harrogate crashed, however, when she saw Millie's pale face and over-bright eyes. Could the girl be tubercular? But she hadn't been coughing. Tonia placed her hand on the white forehead. Not the fever she had feared. If anything Millie was cold, as the slight tremors in her muscles would indicate. "Just a minute, I'll be right back."

Tonia ran down the stairs and snatched a blanket from the pitifully thin stack in the linen cupboard. In her haste she snagged an instrument from the next shelf. It fell to the floor with a clatter. She retrieved it, shaking her head, her child-hood nurse's admonition ringing in her ears, 'Haste makes waste.'

She replaced the tool which she now saw to be a lancet, next to pair of small scales with weights on the shelf containing Mrs. Beeton's required medical appliances: a probe, a pair of forceps and some curved needles. An ounce and drachm measure-glass sat on a lower shelf next to a small wooden chest. The attractive carving of the polished wood attracted Tonia's attention. She reached to lift the lid, but discovered the case was locked. She wondered briefly what specialized tool it held, but took no more time to investigate.

"There now, that will have you warmer soon." She tucked the blanket securely around Millie, then stroked her shoulder, just as she would have done Charlie. Indeed, as she did nightly, for in the eight months since his birth she had never once failed in her regular visits to her son's nursery.

"Thank 'ee." Millie's voice was weak; her eyes darted around the room.

"What else can I do for you, Millie? A drink of water? No, some nice hot tea? The soup isn't ready yet."

"No drink," Millie declared with surprising firmness. Then her voice lowered to a whisper, requiring Tonia to bend her ear to the girl's mouth. "Poison. I saw..."

"What did you see? Who did you see?"

"The man. The same one. 'E'll come again. 'E's everywhere." She tossed her head from side to side on the pillow, looking wildly around the room. Was the girl hallucinating?

"There's no one here, Millie. Who do you see? Freddie? Hardy?"

Millie shook her head and muttered something Tonia couldn't fully hear that sounded like "Dark Street," but that made no sense. The girl was raving. It broke Tonia's heart. She had so wanted to help this one family. With all the suffering around them, she had hoped to do good for this one little clutch of orphans. No wonder Freddie was despondent.

One thing she could do for Millie, though, she could make another visit to the ragged school. Hopefully she would have news to cheer her patient.

"Try to rest, Millie. Cece will bring you some soup when it's ready. You trust her, don't you?"

Millie nodded.

"And I'll go visit Joey and Flossie and the others. That will make you feel better won't it?" This time Millie's nod was accompanied by a small smile.

Danvers insisted on escorting his wife. And she insisted they take a hackney, claiming that she was fatigued, knowing he would resist any concession to his own comfort.

"Wot?" Louisa answered their insistent knock with her usual frown. "Oh, it's you lot, is it? Wot's tha mean plaguin' us all t' time? We keep strict rules 'ere, we do. Don't 'ave no time for no toffy noses stickin' their 'igh an' mightiness in."

She started to close the door, but Danvers stuck his walking stick, which he had consented to carry, inside the frame and pushed the door open wide with his left hand. Tonia swept into the dark entry, remembering to hold her breath. But now that they were in, what would they do? If Louisa remained obdurate how would they find Flossie and the others?

"We've come to call on Miss Flossie Carter. You will be kind enough to direct us to her." Danvers's voice spoke the breeding of generations of ruling class.

"She's scrubbin'." Louisa jerked her head in the direction from which the smell of stale cooking odors, mingled with whatever else, indicated the dining hall.

When they stepped inside the room filled with long, bare tables and wooden benches they saw several girls on their knees, wielding scrub brushes and rags on the wide, grimy floorboards. It was only a moment until one of them dropped her brush with a cry of delight and ran to Tonia. Tonia hugged her as she knew Millie would have done. "Flossie, why are you scrubbing? You're supposed to be having lessons. Have they taught you your letters yet?"

"Mr. Pimm sez it's industrial trainin', so's we can be maids." She looked at her work-roughened hands. More like those of an old crone than a young girl.

"But what of reading?" Tonia persisted.

Flossie hesitated, took a deep breath and plunged, "A, Bae, Cee, D..." She faltered.

"Well, that's a start. So you do have lessons?"

Flossie looked over shoulder at a girl whose grey orphan dress hung on her thin shoulders, her pale hair straggling in her eyes as she applied her scrub brush. "Mary Amelia, she told me letters when she was sick. A'fore she took too poorly. Cassy tried. But she were taken."

"Taken? You mean she got adopted?" What a hopeful thought that these children might be taken into loving homes.

"Nah. By t' reaper."

"Oh, you mean she died?"

Flossie nodded.

"I'm so sorry," Tonia said.

Flossie shrugged. "'Appens, don't it?"

"'Ere now. That's quite enough." Louisa charged into the room. "Back to work, thee."

Flossie turned like a frightened rabbit, but Tonia stopped her. "Wait. How are Joey and the others? Millie will want to know."

But Flossie had skittered back to her scrub brush. Louisa answered. "'E's farmin'. Mr. Pimm, in 'is generosity, found 'im a place."

"And the others? Tim, Sukey, Lettie?" Tonia insisted.

"Useless brats. Too little fer proper work." Tonia was certain Louisa would have shoved her toward the door had she dared.

Flossie raised her head as Tonia walked by. Her voice was so soft she wasn't certain, but it sounded as though she said, "Sukey's sick."

Tonia hadn't thought anything could be grimmer than thinking about the madness and murder of the Dove trial, but back in the cab, she found her mind returning to the trial almost as an escape to dwelling on the misery of the orphans at the York Industrial Ragged School.

"What did you think of the trial this morning, Charles? Do you believe Dove mad?"

"I do. That part of the matter seems to be irrefutable. Bliss was just blowing smoke in suggesting that the poisoning was accidental or that Harriet died of hysterics, although I'll say he made the best argument he could for his client. It's obvious the thrust of his defense is that the man is insane and therefore not responsible for his actions."

Tonia nodded, the question running around and around in her mind almost too deep to voice. At last she asked, "But what of the outcome? Should someone be relieved of the guilt of murder if they are mad?"

"That is for the jury—and probably ultimately Bramwell —to decide. The decision is certain to be a most significant one for the future. The jury decides guilt, which I can't imagine they could fail to find. It remains for the judge to sentence."

Clearly, that was how it would work. That was the justice system. And England's was the finest in the world. But what did that mean to the victims of such crimes? To their families?

Antonia continued to ponder all the way back to Wandseley hall. What of the victims of other such crimes? She thought of Polly who died in that very house just a few nights ago. And of the dead women at the Magdalen Asylum. Was Victoria right in thinking the cause of their deaths unnatural? Could the death of Harriet Dove and the Magdalen women be connected? If so, surely this was the work of a madman.

William Dove, mad or not, was securely locked up in York Castle Prison, but was a madman stalking the streets of York? Even the halls of The Magdalen asylum? Of Wandseley Hall?

❧ 18 ❧

Tonia couldn't have been happier to leave such morbid thoughts behind her the next morning when, at first light, they gathered at Andrewgate around the corner from the Magdalen House where Hardy was filling the aerostat with gas. "Cece, how charming you look," she greeted their young charge, approving of her soft blue poplin travelling dress, its small collar adorned with two rows of plaited cambric. And noting that Cecilia had, in accord with Tonia's instructions, chosen a narrow-brimmed bonnet and left her crinoline off, for two ladies in wide-brimmed bonnets and full crinolines would more than fill the gondola.

Antonia felt her spirits rise with the ascent of the red and yellow striped aerostat and sensed that the mood of the others lightened as well. The morning had begun with a note of disappointment. Tonia had carefully planned time to visit Charlie in his nursery before setting out on their outing, but the early hour set for departure meant that the infant wasn't yet awake when she tiptoed into the nursery, hoping to catch his lovely first-waking smile which was always like the sunshine appearing from behind a cloud bank. The darling infant had been sleeping so soundly, however, he didn't even stir when she ran her fingers through his tousled fair curls, so she had to content herself with merely planting the softest of kisses on his velvet forehead.

But now she could take pleasure in the mid-July sun shining on the green fields beyond the city walls and the slight westerly breeze wafting them straight toward Harrogate. "Due west, Hardy. Hardly any need to take readings," Danvers said, returning his compass to his pocket. "Good, stiff breeze. We should cover the twenty miles to Harrogate in something over an hour." The fact that he then chose to sit on the small stool Hardy had placed in the gondola assured Antonia more than anything else of the rightness of her urging him to take the waters. She noted, but didn't comment on the fact that he had chosen to carry his stick today as well.

They soon left the River Ouse and the walls of the city behind them and floated out over the wide, flat Vale of York, a patchwork of shades of green, some of them turning golden with ripening corn. Cows and sheep grazed in the grasslands and darker patches of conifers marked distant ridges.

"Oh, this is famous! It's like being a bird. I had no idea." Cecilia hung over the edge of the gondola in her fascination.

"Be careful, Cece, don't lean too far over." Antonia held her by the arm, drawing her back from the edge.

A farmer in his field looked up and waved as they floated over him. Tonia and Cece both waved back. Cece was quite right, it was delightful. Tonia removed her bonnet, allowing the breeze to cool her head. Of course, her main objective was to allow Charles to observe that the rusty apricot shade of her new travelling dress exactly matched her hair when the sun shone on it.

His appreciative smile told her that her efforts had not been in vain.

"Look, there's the River Nidd," Cecilia pointed to a tree-lined meandering river below them.

Hardy consulted his map. "Aye, and that'll be Knaresborough—just there." He pointed to a collection of buildings around a town square, a ruined castle and a Norman church along the banks of the river.

They flew over a thickly wooded area, birds flying up from the trees to greet them, to Cece's added delight. Soon the farms and green parkland gave way to scattered houses. The housing became denser and more carriages filled the road below them, which they had followed for most of the journey.

Danvers pointed to a green field not far off the road. "That should do very nicely, Hardy. I trust my brother has secured the services of a carriage and has already spotted our imminent arrival."

Hardy began valving and in a short time they bumped to the ground, only to be taken back up again by a sudden breeze. Hardy valved again, allowing sufficient gas to escape this time that the aerostat remained on land. Hardy was over the side in a moment, securing the gondola and it's partially deflated balloon to the ground with grappling hooks. Danvers was next over the side and the men handed the ladies out.

That was no sooner accomplished than a fine open landau pulled by a pair of perfectly matched greys veered off the road and followed a rutted track across the field toward them. "Well arrived!" Frederick jumped off the driver's seat where he had apparently been sitting to direct the coachman in following the aerostat.

Tonia blinked. How refreshing to see Freddie in a well-cut dark suit, fashionable high collar and cravat again, rather than the clericals he usually wore. She had forgotten how very striking he was. She smiled. And how very much he looked like Charles when first she fell in love with him.

Freddie turned back to the carriage, opened the door and held out his hand. A young woman put her hand in his and emerged from the folds of the seat. "Vicky!" Cecilia shouted and dashed forward. The two girls embraced, exchanging exclamations as if they had been apart for months rather than for a few days. At last Cecilia drew her sister forward to renew her acquaintance with Lord and Lady Danvers. It was startling to see the twin sisters together; they looked so much alike, in spite of Cecilia's obviously more robust health.

Victoria was still unnaturally pale, but her golden ringlets shone from around the blue ribbons of her bonnet and her voice held a charming musical quality as she welcomed the newcomers to Harrogate and explained the accommodation Frederick had secured for them at the Swan Inn. "I do hope you will find it adequate, Lady Danvers; it's where my father always insists on staying. I think it has memories for him—of staying there with our mother. It's one of the first inns built in Harrogate. At that time High Harrogate was the most fashionable, although when they discovered the stinking wells and built the pump room, Low Harrogate became more fashionable."

Tonia realized the girl, in her gentle way, was apologizing that their rooms weren't in the height of fashion. She laughed and took her hand. "My dear, I'm sure your father's choice will be most adequate. I can't imagine that we would prefer accommodation near any place called the stinking wells."

"It's the sulfur, you know. It's part of what makes the waters so effective, but they are rather, er—well, odiferous." Vicky gave a brief, almost mischievous smile.

It wasn't until they were settled in the landau with the sisters sitting across from herself and Charles that Tonia realized. At first she thought that Victoria's frequent shy glances upward at Frederick, sitting once again on the driver's seat, were simply an interest in the direction of their journey. Then it struck her. Actually, it had been obvious at their first meeting, but she hadn't paid sufficient attention.

The fact of the matter was that this lovely, delicate young girl couldn't keep her eyes off Frederick. Victoria was in love with Freddie, the clergyman who had declared himself called to celibacy. *Oh, my*, Tonia thought and bit her lip. *What a state of affairs.* Surely the last thing anyone wanted was for Victoria to get her heart broken. And yet, what possible other outcome was there?

❧ 19 ❧

Was Victoria ill or merely pining for Frederick? It was certainly obvious to Tonia that Selina, Victoria's watchdog maid, blamed Freddie. Tonia had observed the maid with her iron-grey hair and ice-blue eyes glaring at him. "Will you be staying long, sir?" the maid inquired stiffly.

"Only a few hours, I'm afraid. Have to return tonight." His answer doused the light in Victoria's eyes.

But Tonia was certain she heard Selina mutter, "And a good thing, too."

"But we intend to spend every moment to advantage." Tonia gave Vicky a bright smile, hoping it didn't look forced. "Now, tell us what we are to do."

"The routine is quite established," Victoria informed them. "One must arrive at the pump Room before nine o'clock every morning. My doctor would have me drink two glasses, but one is often all I can manage." She turned to Danvers, looking at him shyly through her long eyelashes. "Don't let me alarm you. It isn't too terrible. Not if you remember to hold your breath while drinking. Many people consume as much as a quart at a time.

"Then fifteen minutes of promenade in the Assembly Rooms. That's most essential for the..." She fumbled to a stop, realizing she was in polite company.

Tonia's imagination supplied the word 'purge' and she hastened to the girl's rescue. "Of course, my dear. We shall accompany you directly." She gave Danvers a challenging look. "I avow I'll be able to drink more than you, my lord."

In spite of her dare, Antonia insisted that they be taken to their hotel first so that Isabella could assist her in tightening her stays and donning her crinoline. Lady Antonia Danvers had no intention of promenading in one of the most fashionable spas in England, perhaps in all of Europe, with skirts falling short of the prescribed fashionable width.

In spite of the detour, however, they arrived at the attractive, domed Pump Room building across from the tree and flower-filled park comfortably before the required hour. When Antonia caught her first whiff of the sulfur springs, however, she felt she had perhaps been a bit rash in declaring a contest as to the amount she could consume.

The sulfuric smell took her back instantly to less than two years before when she had sought the curative powers of similar waters at Tunbridge Wells. And the birth of their cherished son had been the result. She could only hope Harrogate's waters would have equally restorative effects for its drinkers.

Danvers tipped the pumper for all the party to have a sample of the water and managed to down a full glass. Antonia, however, even though she held her breath, could swallow only half of hers. Whether the iron and sulfur concentration was stronger in these waters than those at Tunbridge Wells or whether she was simply lacking the urgent motive that had driven her before, she was uncertain, but she set her unemptied glass on the small table with a chagrined smile at her husband and turned her attention to the fashionable company filling the gracefully ornamented room. Its soft green walls beneath the curved ceiling were accented by cream moldings and pilasters. An ornate stained glass window, featuring pictures of an angel, swan and water lilies filled the wall above the pump.

Victoria was the champion, emptying the two glasses prescribed for her. Antonia was uncertain whether the bloom she saw in the girl's cheeks was because the chalybeate waters were finally having their effect or because Frederick praised her efforts.

"The waters seem to be doing you good," Tonia remarked to Vicky.

"Yes, I do believe so. I was worried because I had finished the last of the tonic I brought with me and I feared I would flag, but the iron and sulfur in these waters seem to be quite efficacious."

After the regulation drinks their party strolled up the tree-lined, cobbled street to a restaurant for breakfast. Since she had been up for hours in the fresh air and had taken only chocolate and toast at Wandseley Hall, Antonia was more than ready to enjoy the meal. She ordered her favorite kedgeree and savored the combination of fish, rice and eggs in a mustard sauce.

Victoria and Cecilia were just settling which of the shops they should visit first when Hardy entered the restaurant and bounded across the room to them. "It's all settled, my lord, booked you are for the full treatment: hydrotherapy, massage and galvanism." He waved a pamphlet written by a Doctor Isaiah Pritchard of the Galvanic Hydrotherapy Institute. "I read all the pamphlets offered by all the wells, my lord. I can assure you this is the most thorough. You won't be regretting it."

Danvers scowled. "I believe that to be highly unlikely, Hardy, as I am regretting it already." But he consented to follow his man.

Antonia awaited his return to The Swan with some anxiety. Surely bathing in potent mineral waters, waters treated with electricity, even, followed by a vigorous massage would do Charles a world of good. After all, people came from long distances for such treatments and there was great medical testimony to their benefits. Yet, back in their room, Tonia found herself pacing the floor and twisting her handkerchief as she waited.

At last she heard his footstep on the hall. A less uneven step than since his injury, perhaps? Danvers stopped just inside the door to their suite. "Tonia, you look so worried. Has something happened?"

She forced a small laugh. "No, I was concerned for you."

As an answer he crossed the room in three strides and swept her into his arms. "There, does that answer your question?"

"Most adequately, my lord."

And yet as they sat over the tea tray Hardy brought to the room, Tonia found she was having difficulty keeping a note of wistfulness out of her voice. "What is it?" Danvers leaned forward, concern knitting his brows.

Tonia couldn't quite suppress the small sigh that escaped her lips. "I rather hate to admit it, but, in spite of the charms of the spa, I'm afraid I am missing Charlie quite dreadfully. Drinking that vile water today brought back all the longing and waiting and, even despair, of thinking I would never be able to present you with the heir you so deserve."

"And you've never been away from him for so long," he finished for her.

She nodded. "Thank you for understanding." Afternoon was beginning to draw toward evening and she was feeling the familiar tug to visit their adored son. Their unexpected adventures and taking on of charity work in York had kept her far busier than usual and she had spent far less time with Charlie than normal. But she had never spent a whole day without some time spent cuddling and doting on him. Her arms began to ache.

"What if he's missing me?" Then she thought—*what if he doesn't miss me?* That would be worse.

Danvers looked at the ornate gilt clock on the mantle. "There should be just time, my love. If we go now I believe we can meet Hardy at the gas main outside the Pump Room. I always think evening ascents are the most pleasant anyway."

"But your hydrotherapy tomorrow?"

"Do you mind travelling with Freddie? Hardy can return for me after the good Doctor Pritchard has had his way with me."

Even then the decision to return to Wandseley Hall that very evening was a wrenching one. She would have loved to spend more time in the charming spa town with Charles, but as the shadows lengthened she found herself seated in the gondola next to Freddie while the aerostat floated in a meandering pattern, directed by Hardy's intricate valving and adjusting of flaps, back toward York.

She suspected Charles was missing his son as well. The thought brought a soft smile to her face as she leaned against the side of the gondola and thought back over the day. How right she had been to urge her husband to seek the restorative waters. And he must have agreed, notwithstanding his refusal to admit it, because, in spite of his complaints about the acrid sulfur smell, he had submitted to the advice of the attendant doctor that the treatment must continue at least two more days.

"Antonia?" She started at Freddie's voice. Looking out over the side of the gondola the towers and pinnacles of York Minster rose below them and she saw that her ruminations had brought her back to York. And then she realized that not only had she been deep in thought, but Frederick, too, had been silent their entire journey. Not only silent, but in something of a brown study as well.

"Freddie, are you troubled? You look worried."

He put her off with a vague reply, but his pensiveness continued after Hardy brought the Aerostat to a smooth descent and Freddie escorted her across the field to Wandseley hall. She fairly flew up the stairs to the nursery. "Charlie, dearest, did you miss—" She stopped abruptly as Nurse Bevans looked up from the cot with her finger to her lips.

"I'm so sorry, m'lady." She crossed the room to Antonia. "I didn't want him to feel lonesome for you, you see, so I kept him very busy. After his nap we went for a ride in the donkey cart—a lovely drive all along the fields. He did so love the sheep—the little darling. But he was ready for his cot sharp after supper. Of course, if I'd known you'd be returning so soon—"

Antonia, hiding her disappointment, assured Bevans she had done the right thing and contented herself for the second time that day with merely kissing her sleeping son.

She had just descended the stairs when Sir Gerald entered the foyer dressed for going out. "Ah, Lady Danvers. As my wife and the Dowager Duchess haven't returned from the Castle yet, I thought I'd just look in on the last of the trial. Would you care to go with me?"

Antonia, much relieved at not having to spend the evening alone, accepted with alacrity.

The sun was sinking in the west, leaving a pink tinge to the sky behind the Castle, as they drove up Tower Street, the horses' hooves and wheels of the carriage clattering on the cobbles. Occasional carriages coming down the street suggested that, due to the lateness of the hour, a few of the observers had abandoned William Dove to his fate and were going home to their dinner. It meant that Antonia and Sir Gerald should be able to find seats in the courtroom. As it was now nearing nine o'clock, Tonia marveled at the stamina of the Dowager Duchess and the others who assuredly had now been there for more than twelve hours with only short breaks for refreshment.

The bailiff's man opened the heavy oak door to the courtroom for Sir Gerald and bowed to the magistrate. "Well into the judge's summing up, they are." The usher drew out a pocket watch and consulted it. "Five hours he's been going." The man was obviously missing the sausages on toast his good wife would surely have waiting for him.

Baron Bramwell's deep voice boomed into the anteroom, apparently in reply to a question from the defense. "And you, Mr. Bliss, might have asked any question you pleased respecting the prisoner's alleged insanity from the medical witnesses called by the prosecution."

Bliss replied as Tonia and Sir Gerald slipped into seats near the back of the room, "But they were not experts in madness, my lord."

Bramwell nearly exploded at the counsel, "Experts in madness! Mad doctors! Gentlemen, I will read you the evidence of these medical witnesses—these 'experts in madness.' And if you can make sane evidence out of what they say, then do so; but I confess it's more than I can do."

The judge then reminded the jury that Dr. Caleb Williams, the medical attendant of the Retreat Lunatic Asylum, testified that if a man nourishes any passion until it becomes uncontrollable, that is moral insanity and the accused was then not responsible for his acts.

"I ask you, gentlemen of the jury," The judged leaned forward over the bench so as to address the jury more directly, "Why, if this theory were correct, Dr. Williams should not be called upon, when a man was placed at the bar after two or three convictions for felony, to prove that there must not be a conviction, on the ground that the thief had a delusion in regard to the rights of property, had a propensity to rob the public at large, an uncontrollable impulse to appropriate the property of others, to steal everything in general, and was therefore morally insane and not criminally responsible for his acts?

"Further, you heard the proprietor of a Leeds lunatic asylum Dr. George Pyemont Smith, give the astounding testimony that the non-possession of poison might have made the prisoner refrain from this crime. You know, gentlemen of the jury, I really think you might have known for yourselves, without Dr. Smith bothering himself to come all the way from Leeds to tell you, that if the prisoner had no poison in his possession he could not have poisoned his wife.

"Dr. Smith also told you that the prisoner knew right from wrong during the fatal week, but the temptation to commit the crime was too strong. I ask you, is not this the case with all criminals? Do not they all commit crimes because the temptation is stronger than their fear of the penal consequences?

"If the theory of these gentlemen were true of the prisoner, it would be equally true in the case of every criminal and form a conclusive reason for liberating every person charged with crime.

"It is now in your hands, gentlemen. It is for you to take the whole of the evidence together—the facts which have been proved, the opinions which have been given, the arguments which have been used—it is for you to take all these things into your serious consideration, and, having well and solemnly weighed them, to say in your judgment and according to the best of your belief, was the prisoner conscious that the act was one which he ought not to commit, and had he sufficient reason to know that what he was doing was wrong. I have laid before you, to the best of my ability, the law. You, gentlemen, are the sole judges to decide the guilt or innocence of the prisoner."

Escorted by the bailiff, the jury left the room. Tonia turned her attention again to the man standing in the dock. She found it amazing that throughout these grueling days his appearance and manner were entirely unchanged. She saw still the same imperturbable demeanor, the same quiet attention to all going forward in the court and the perfect ease and self-possession which he had maintained throughout.

Sir Gerald looked at his pocket watch. It was five minutes past ten o'clock. The creak and shuffle of feet and rustle of fabric that immediately filled the courtroom was quickly drowned in the buzz of speculation as everyone expressed his or her opinion or solicited their neighbor's views. Tonia wondered how long the jury would be out. She had risen at dawn that morning and, come to think of it, had eaten nothing since the cucumber sandwiches and shortbread she had shared with Charles hours ago. She closed her eyes and let the babble swirl around her.

She didn't have long to wait, however, for little more than half an hour later the jury returned. The Clerk of Arraigns called each juror's name and each answered "present."

"Gentleman of the Jury," The Clerk continued, "have you agreed upon your verdict?"

The foreman, who had earlier answered to the name of Mr. Hewitt, rose. "We have."

"How say you, guilty or not guilty?"

Hewitt cleared his throat and responded in a ringing tone. "Guilty." He paused. "But we recommend him to mercy on the ground of defective intellect."

The Clerk turned to the prisoner. "William Dove, you have been convicted of the crime of murder."

Dove started to speak, but was cut off at a call for silence. Tonia felt she could almost hear the intake of breath before the hush that followed as if all held their breath. All except the journalists. The scratching of pencils and the rustle of paper filling the gallery evidenced their frenzy of activity.

Baron Bramwell placed a small black cap atop his wig and looked directly at William Dove. Tonia was amazed when Bramwell began to speak that his voice held so much emotion. "Prisoner at the bar, you have been found guilty of the crime laid to your charge. You have been guilty of murder —the most dreadful of all crimes and by the most odious of all modes—by poison. It was murder, I fear, committed under circumstances of the greatest deliberation."

Bramwell, apparently overcome by the awesome responsibility that was his, took a deep breath and continued, in a voice so soft it was difficult to hear, speaking directly to the prisoner, "The jury, in my judgment, have done their duty to their country and to their consciences. They have done their duty in repelling the kind of defense which has been made for you—that your mind was in such a condition that you were not to be held responsible for the consequences of your acts. I have no doubt that you were responsible.

"At the same time, the jury have yielded to their natural impulses in recommending to show mercy to one upon the state of whose mind there had been so much said. That recommendation shall be forwarded to the proper quarter, and, if acquiesced in, will be extended to you.

"But be prepared to find it rejected." Again he paused.

"I shall pass sentence upon you—not my sentence, but

that of the law. And as you have but a short time to live, I recommend you to employ that time in preparation for the fate which is before you. I have no doubt that you have a capacity—an ample mental capacity—for a knowledge of religious truths, and I doubt not that you may profitably employ the time left to you in considering them and in seeking that spiritual advice and assistance which will be offered to you.

"My duty now is to pass upon you the solemn sentence of the law. That sentence, and the sentence of this court, is that, for the crime of willful murder, you be taken hence to the prison from whence you came, and thence to the place of execution, and there hanged by the neck till your body be dead.

"And may the Lord have mercy upon your soul."

Even from the back of the room, Tonia could see the prisoner's features quiver with emotion at the pronouncement of the dread sentence. He appeared for a second as if intending to speak. Tonia held her breath. What could one say after hearing those words spoken over their head?

After a moment's hesitation, however, Dove turned sharply and descended the stairs at the back of the dock. A sense of release flooded the room. A sharp exhale of breath was followed immediately with a hubbub of chatter and patter of feet as people rose and moved toward the door. First to exit, though, were the journalists, rushing from the gallery, elbowing all in their way, and scrambling out the door to get to their newspapers.

Tonia, too, let out a long sigh, realizing suddenly how very exhausted she was. It had been a day of emotions and sensations, of questions answered and unanswered, but she could cope with none of it at the moment.

She turned to Sir Gerald, "Take me home, I pray you." She was unspeakably grateful for the support of his strong arm to lead her from the room.

20

Tonia felt only the briefest pang of guilt the next morning for allowing herself to sleep till midmorning and miss church. She knew Sir Gerald and Philomena would be faithful in their attendance at their parish church and Freddie would have valued her attendance at St. Alphege's, but that duty would have to await another day. Today was to be wholly devoted to her son. "Isabella, you may bring my breakfast to me in the nursery. I shall join Charlie for his midmorning repast."

Before she could escape to the nursery, however, the door to Tonia's room was flung back and the Dowager Duchess entered. "Aunt Aelfrida, I'm amazed you're about so early."

"Early? Nonsense, gel, it's 11 o'clock. I've already been to matins. Why didn't I see you in the breakfast room? I'm most anxious to discuss this with you." She waved the newspaper she carried folded in her hand.

Tonia's heart sank. She was aching to be with Charlie. "Won't you sit down, Aunt Aelfrida?"

Since the Dowager Duchess was already halfway to one of the mauve and mulberry striped satin chairs sitting before the

Adam fireplace, there was little doubt as to the answer to Tonia's invitation. "So what do you think? Was Dove mad or excessively wicked?"

Tonia opened her mouth to say it seemed to her that his actions had shown an excess of both. But apparently Aunt Aelfrida's question was merely rhetorical. "Evil, no doubt of it. Brought up in a well-to-do, pious household, offered a good education—a cruel boy that became a vicious murderer."

She tapped her walking stick against the leg of the chair for emphasis. "Although I will allow it was clearly understood in my day that Methodistical enthusiasm provoked insanity—an alarming rise in madness among evangelical fanatics was well known. Still, a brain fevered by ranting preachers is hardly an excuse for murdering one's wife.

"The papers are full of 'moral insanity' this morning." She scoffed. "Whatever that is supposed to mean." She read from her paper, "'His actions were not merely those of a wicked, vicious or eccentric man, but they evidently sprang out of a stunted, irregularly developed, congenitally defective and badly organized brain and mind.'

"What else would they expect from one who had sold himself to the devil, I ask you?"

Tonia merely shook her head, as the Dowager Duchess continued. Tonia knew better than to attempt an answer, even if she had one. "What of free will and personal responsibility? Those are the underpinnings of civilized society. If everyone could be excused of murder on the ground of a 'disorganized mind' what basis would be left for civilization? We might as well turn our prisons into health spas."

Isabella entered with a tray of tea and toast, for which Tonia was most grateful, but Aelfrida waved her offered cup away. Tonia took that moment to insert, "It's so desperately sad. Poor Harriet. Bramwell did very well to stress the odiousness of poison and especially its use against the wife under Dove's protection—the wife whom he had sworn to love and care for."

"Quite right. Just as these new laws against wife-beating substantiate. Only occurs in the lower orders, of course, but that's just the point—it is our responsibility to keep the lower orders in line."

Tonia weighed the consequences of reminding Aelfrida that Dove was of good middle class stock, as she herself had said, but Tonia's mind was back on her own responsibility to those less fortunate. What of the poor women who had died so suddenly under her care? If they had been poisoned as appeared, wouldn't it have had to be by someone from the 'upper orders'?

Surely none of the unfortunate inhabitants of Bedern would have had reason or opportunity to administer any fatal dose to those hapless women. She must quiz Freddie and Carlotta more carefully as to their volunteers. Was someone working in the Magdalen House as mad or as bad as William Dove?

Happily The Dowager Duchess took her silence as agreement. "I am most gratified to see your understanding is quite correct in this matter." She rose. "You may remove the tray," she directed Isabella.

Tonia laughed at the look of confused astonishment on her maid's face as the door closed behind her visitor. "Most certainly, Isabella." She returned her half-eaten toast triangle to the tray. "Take it away. Countermanding the Dowager Duchess is more than my head would be worth. But you may bring me a fresh one in the nursery. I shall spend the rest of the day with my son."

A delightful day it was, too, for both mother and son, so that by Monday morning Antonia felt refreshed and invigorated to approach the problems of Magdalen House with renewed energy. And really, she must do so if she were to solve the matter for Freddie. That morning's post had brought a heartening report from Bracken recounting the excellent progress of the rebuilding at Norwood. Soon they would be required there to choose carpets, wall-coverings and new furnishings to replace those lost in the fire.

And, an even more heartening thought—if the succeeding hydrotherapy sessions were as efficacious as the first seemed to be, it would be only a matter of a day or two until Charles would be recovered. The thought brought such lightening to her heart as she and Hardy alighted from the carriage with Philomena Wandseley for their day of charity work that she all but entered the door with a skip.

And cannoned into a sturdy female figure with a bag in each hand. Tonia blinked as her eyes adjusted to the dim light. Who was this woman with the frazzled hair and muscular arms? Surely not one of the women taken in for care. "I beg your pardon." Tonia stepped aside. "Have we met?"

Tonia's query was rebuffed with an offended sniff.

"Isa," Lady Wandseley spoke from behind Tonia. "What are you doing?"

"Leavin' that's wot Ah'm doin'. And not afore time."

"Leaving? But why, Isa?"

Now Tonia remembered. Isa was the night nurse who slept at the back of the house. Tonia had been informed of her presence, but had never met her as the nurse had always been asleep when Tonia was at the asylum.

"Ah'll not stay 'ere to have my name blackened. Poison she said. 'Er lady high-an'-mightiness. Five years Ah've been a nurse. Knew Florence Nightingale in the Crimea, Ah did. Ain't never been accused of no such thing." Isa ended with another sniff and pushed her way through to the door, all but knocking Hardy over as he followed Lady Wandseley.

Tonia rapped on the door of Carlotta Billingston's office. "Come."

"Carlotta, what on earth happened?"

"Oh, you met Isa on her way out, did you?" Carlotta sighed and shook her head. "I warned her. Innumerable times. Well, all nurses drink, don't they? But this was too much. I had to dismiss her. Although I have small enough hope of replacing her with anyone better."

"But she said she was accused of poisoning?" Tonia gasped. "Carlotta, there hasn't been another..."

"No, by the grace of God. But who knows what might have happened if she hadn't been so drunken that she spilled all three bottles." Carlotta indicated three nearly empty tonic bottles on her desk.

Antonia blinked. "Are you saying the tonic is dangerous?" Was Millie right in refusing to take it?

"Of course not, it's a superb restorative, I make it myself, as you well know. But it's intended to be administered by the spoonful—in a glass of water, or used externally. Not to be drunk by the bottle."

"But if Isa was a poisoner shouldn't we call the police?"

"What interest do the police have in incompetence? It's far better to deal with these matters ourselves." She stood in a dismissive manner. "Now, my dear Lady Danvers, if you'll excuse me, I must get on to the agency. If I don't have a replacement by tonight I shall have to ask one of our volunteers to stay over, and I can't imagine anyone agreeing to do that."

As Carlotta swept from the room Tonia was aware of a sense of relief that the answer could be so simple. But was it too simple? Did a drunken night nurse answer for all the seemingly unaccountable deaths under this roof? Tonia regarded the bottles on Carlotta's desk. Could the tonic have been the cause all along as Millie claimed? On impulse she collected the bottles. She could simply tell Carlotta she had tidied them up if asked.

She found Hardy and Freddie setting out the soup bowls in the dining room. "Hardy, can you take these to an apothecary and request an analysis of the ingredients? I know nothing of chemistry, but there must be something they can do to find out what was really in that mixture."

Hardy looked startled, but the bottles disappeared into the capacious pockets of his emerald green coat. "What is this, Tonia? Have you learned something?" Freddie quizzed.

"I don't know. Just a feeling, really. Too many coincidences." That reminded her that she wanted to ask for a list of volunteers.

"Yes, certainly. I'll have it for you this evening. But surely, you don't think—"

"I don't think anything, Freddie. All I have are questions. After all, if Isa was responsible the matter will be at an end."

That hopeful thought returned the spring to Tonia's step as she went upstairs to see Millie and the others. The room was unaccountably quiet. At first she thought it was merely the absence of the deceased Nan's soft moans that had so filled her corner, and the equally incessant complaining from Iris. A glance in the direction of Iris's bed told her its occupant was asleep. Then she realized that the heavily breathing figure was not in Iris's bed, which was empty. Rather, the newcomer was in the bed Nan had occupied. Stepping quietly, she crossed the floor to look at their new patient.

She drew back, suppressing a gasp, at the sight of the ugly bruises and lacerations covering the woman's skin. One eye was bandaged, the other, not closed in sleep as Tonia had thought, but staring despondently into the gloom.

And Iris's bed was empty. Tonia turned back to Millie. "What happened?"

"Night Watch brought 'er in. More dead 'an alive. Isa bandaged 'er an' give 'er a sleepin' draught." She shrugged to indicate that was the extent of her knowledge, then added. "Gert, Ah think 'er name is, but 'ard to tell wot she said with so many teeth missin'."

"And Iris?" Tonia asked.

"'Er man come fer 'er."

"Was she strong enough to go?"

Again, Millie shrugged. "'E took 'er."

And that was an end to it, Tonia thought. In spite of the anti wife-beating law Aunt Aelfrida had spoken of with such complacency, the fact of the matter was that a wife was still considered her husband's property. To do with as he liked in many quarters. The best she could hope was that Iris could gain her strength before she got with child again. And she hoped the man was her husband rather than her pimp.

At least Betsy and Annie Rose were flourishing, and Millie seemed stronger today. Tonia placed her hand on the sheet over the girl's ballooning abdomen. Surely she would need her strength to deliver her child almost any moment now. "You're doing well, Millie. The food here has been strengthening. Just what you needed."

"Yeh, Ah'm ever so grateful. Don't know what woulda become of us..." She bit her lip.

"You're still worried about the little ones, aren't you?" Millie nodded. Tonia was sure that the girl would need to concentrate on more immediate matters soon. The least she could do would be to put her mind to rest.

"You know I didn't see the others, but Flossie was doing very well when I visited. She's even made a friend." She started to tell her about Cassy, then remembered. Cassy was dead. "I'll go see them." She almost ran from the room.

"Hardy, you must come with me. We need to go see Flossie." Tonia didn't understand the impulse that seized her, but she didn't want to waste time analyzing it. She was simply certain that something more than slothful mismanagement was wrong at the ragged school.

"Tha's 'ere again?" Louisa started to close the door but Hardy had his hand on it and he was stronger.

Fear gripped Tonia's heart as she marched toward the end of the hall where she saw a small group of girls on their hands and knees around a pale of dirty water. What if Flossie wasn't here? What if she had been 'took' like Cassy? Or what of Sukey. She recalled Floss's whispered words: *Sukey's sick.*

"Flossie, thank God." The girl looked thin and haggard, but no more so than usual. "How's Sukey?"

Flossie nodded, but before she could answer, Louisa clamped a rough hand on Antonia's arm. "'Ere now, thee stop bargin' in 'ere disturbin' our students or Ah'll go fer t' coppers."

"Yes, and I'm thinking that would be a fine thing to do." Hardy put a guiding hand on Louisa's shoulder to move her away from Antonia. "Matter o' fact, let me escort you. Lady like you shouldn't be out on the street alone. Rough area, this is." Hardy moved Louisa toward the door like a sheepdog herding his charge.

"'Ere now, just 'old yer 'orses," Louisa protested. "No need ter get all riled up."

Tonia smiled and turned back to Floss. "Is everyone all right?" The girl hung her head. "Flossie, tell me!"

"We're awreet, lady. Truly. T' work's fierce 'ard an' t' gruel's thin, but it's reg'lar. 'S better'n bein' on t' street."

Tonia sensed there was something the girl was holding back. "But what's wrong?" She urged.

"'S Ilene. She took Cass's bed next to mine. Two nights ago. She coughed all night. Next mornin' there was blood on 'er pillow where she coughed. An' she were gone."

Tonia hugged the girl. Was that three of Flossie's friends in the short time she had been here? And in these dreadful conditions it was little wonder. Flossie said it was better than being on the street, but Tonia wondered. At least the air was marginally fresher outside. "Are you beaten? Mistreated?" But even as Flossie denied such treatment Tonia wondered what could constitute mistreatment worse than what was apparent to the eye.

Back at the doorway she heard Hardy and Louisa arguing with loud voices. Tonia smiled. Hardy could match anyone insult for insult, threat for threat. Just beyond where the girls were scrubbing, she spied an open door. She moved forward to investigate. It was apparently Pimm's office. Louisa must have left the door open when she went out to answer their insistent knock. Tonia gazed around in the poor light, unsure what she hoped to find. Could Pimm be using the children to steal? Or selling the girls? Even the boys? Wild schemes flitted through Tonia's mind. If so what sort of evidence might she find here?

A stack of unpaid bills littered the desk, but they didn't seem to be far in arrears. The account book was open on the desk. Tonia glanced at the figures. Hard to tell at such a cursory glance, but she could see nothing obviously amiss. She opened the top drawer. Quills, a pen knife, letter opener, powder for mixing ink... It was surprisingly in order. The next drawer seemed to contain settled accounts. Who would have thought the slovenly Pimm to be so tidy about his accounts?

Tonia closed the drawer and moved to go when an enormous thud at her feet made her start. She didn't see anything and started to move forward when her toe struck an object and almost tripped her. If she hadn't grabbed the edge of the desk she would have plunged forward.

Moving her skirt aside she realized what had happened. The wide sleeve of her dress had caught a large book sitting on the corner of the desk, knocking it to the floor, and her crinoline had covered it as she moved forward. She picked up the heavy volume and began to replace it when she saw what it was. The register of children brought into the York Industrial Ragged School.

In neat columns in Pimm's surprisingly clear handwriting each child was entered with their age and the date they were brought into the school. Yes, here they were: 8 July 1856; Carter—Joey, Floss, Tim, Sukey, Lettie. Quite in order. Tonia started to close the volume when a name at the top of the page caught her eye. Unusual because few slum children were given names like Mary Amelia. Wasn't that the girl Flossie told her about? The one who taught her letters before she died? And yet the name was not crossed off to indicate that Mary Amelia was no longer with them.

Tonia scanned the rest of the page. Ilene, the last name before the bottom was registered as having entered two days before, but, again, not marked through. What was the name of that other girl? The one who had 'been taken'? Callie? She looked further back in the list. No, here it was, Cassy. Still, as far as the record indicated, hail and thriving in the school.

Tonia had no idea what it meant, but she knew it wasn't right. "I'll sling the both o' yuz out!" Louisa's voice sounded louder, making Tonia jump. She slipped out the door, past the scrubbing girls and down the hallway. Whatever it was, she had done all she could do here.

All the way back to Wandseley Hall Tonia longed for Charles. If only he were here he would know what to make of the mystery. She could think of only one thing to do. She went straight to Sir Gerald's study and rapped on his door with more impatience than she intended. "Yes. Lady Danvers, do come in. Has my wife returned with you?"

"No, she's still at the asylum. Hardy secured a hackney for me. I've found—" She paused for breath. "I don't know what I've found, but I must have advice."

"But, of course, sit down, my dear. May I ring for refreshment for you?"

"No, thank you." She launched into her story, telling him about Millie coming to the refuge and their taking her five young siblings to the ragged school.

"Yes," Sir Gerald nodded. "A wise decision. I'm on the board of the corporation for the school. A fine vision to get orphans off the street, teach them their letters and fit them for useful employment. A model, if I do say so myself. One I can only hope other cities might emulate."

"Well, Sir Gerald, if I might speak frankly—"

"But of course, please do."

She told him of the apparent lack of instruction, the poor food and the work forced on the children.

He frowned. "Of course the work scheme is part of the program. They must work if they are to learn a trade.'

"A trade, yes, but surely not sweeping chimneys?" Wandseley looked startled, but Tonia realized she had strayed from her most immediate concern. She told him of the three girls she knew had died by Flossie's personal account and yet their names remained on the record as still enrolled.

Sir Gerald sat back in his high leather chair, his hands folded over his considerable girth. "Hmm. I wonder... I fear we might have been most woefully remiss. Pimm came to us with excellent recommendations, you see, so we rather let him get on with the running of his school. He is known to be most vigorous in combing the slums and collecting orphans.

But perhaps..." He stroked the ample mutton chop running down his cheek. "Yes, I think I see."

"What is it, Sir Gerald? Are the Carter children in danger?"

"I wouldn't think so. Not from unnatural causes if that's what you're suggesting. But I see the flaw in the accounting the corporation requires of Pimm. He's paid, you see—well paid—by the church per pupil. They give Christian burial to children who die. The corporation sees that as an important part of our duty. It's a sad fact of life that more orphans die than live. And Pimm loses payment when a child dies."

"But that's wicked. If he is concealing the deaths, the children are denied Christian burial."

"Precisely. I believe a surprise visit is in order." Sir Gerald rang for his carriage.

"Might I suggest," Tonia ventured as she matched her step to his, "That we enlist the aid of the constables of the ward?" She told him of Louisa's bull-like guarding.

"I shall do just that," he agreed. "But surely you don't mean to go with me, Lady Danvers?"

"I am responsible for five of the charges of the school." She stepped in front of him to be handed into the carriage, leaving little room for argument.

Evening shadows falling across the narrow, litter-strewn street and darkening the grubby buildings made the area seem even more sinister than earlier. Tonia held a gloved hand to her nose against the stench of the central gutter running with refuse. It made her think again of the putrid reek of the building she would soon be entering. She put a hand on her stomach to steady it. At least this time she wouldn't be required to face down the odious Louisa by herself. Four strong constables followed in the police van behind them.

Whatever Sir Gerald suspected he might find, he was prepared.

Louisa opened the door to Sir Gerald's peremptory knock with her usual snarl, but the growl died in her throat at the sight of a member of the corporation backed by uniformed policemen. "'E's in 'is office." She jerked her head down the hall. Sir Gerald strode forward followed by the constables.

Louisa glared at Tonia. "Tha brats is that way." She gestured with her head toward the hall where the reek of boiled cabbage told her supper was in progress. "Get 'em out. Nothin' but trouble since they come."

Tonia had been uncertain what she would do, but following Louisa's suggestion and getting the Carter children out seemed an excellent plan. Perhaps they could stay at the Magdalen refuge tonight. Millie would be delighted. Then they would decide what to do after that. She put her hand over her nose and made for the dining hall. How could anyone—even starving orphans—eat with that stench filling the air?

The scraping of tin spoons on metal plates echoed around the room. Tonia found it heartbreaking that a room full of children should be so silent. It testified even more strongly than their gaunt eyes to their overworked, underfed condition. Tonia was uncertain how she would locate Flossie and the others, but Floss saw her and waved. "Come, I'm taking you to Millie," she said, then looked around. "Where are the boys?"

"Joey's still at t' farm. Tim's 'idin'."

"Hiding?" Tonia asked.

"'E 'eard t' bangin' on t' door. Thought it were t' sweep come fer 'im."

"Why would he think that?"

"'E was sent to sweep today. 'E run off. Pimm don't know. Yet."

"You mean he's hiding somewhere in the school?"

Flossie nodded. "Nowhere else to go."

"Well, then, we must find him." Thank goodness they had come in time to rescue the tyke before he was caught and sent to climb like a monkey up a chimney to clear it. She had heard tales of boys panicking halfway up and the sweep lighting a fire under them to make them continue—sometimes resulting in burnt feet, sometimes in death from the smoke.

She eyed the rabbit warren of hallways and doors. Scores of places for a small boy to hide. "You girls take that hallway. And call out to him. He'll likely answer your voice. If you find him come back to the dining room. You can assure him he will not have to sweep a chimney. Ever."

Tonia started down the corridor leading away from the kitchen, hoping the stench would dissipate if she got away from the cooking odors. The first door she opened was a storage cupboard of some sort. As far as she could see it held mostly broken furniture. "Tim? It's all right. We've come to take you to Millie." She waited. No reply. And the only sound she heard was all too easily identifiable as a rat scurrying across the floor. She slammed the door shut.

"Tim," she tried the next one. But surely not even a frightened boy would be hiding in the coal room. She tried another. And another. Was the air really getting more fetid or was it just that she could no longer use her hands to shield her nose?

The next door was locked. Ah, that must mean Tim was in there. He must have found a key and managed to lock himself in. "Tim?" She knocked on the door. "Timmy, it's Lady Antonia. You remember me. I'm Millie's friend." No answer. She knocked again. "Tim, open the door. I'm here to help you."

She put her ear to the door. Not even the scuffle of a rat.

If Tim was in there he must be holding his breath. This whole end of the building was as silent as a tomb.

"Are you needing some help, m'lady?" Tonia turned and saw Sergeant Carlton who had come to Wandseley Hall the night they found Polly. "Yes, do you think you could break this door down? Timmy Carter, a small charge of mine has run off to hide. I think he's in here, but I can't get him to respond."

"Argh, fair reeks, don't it?" Sergeant Carlton made a face. "Stand aside, m'lady."

Three sharp kicks on the hinges with his heavy police boot and the door swung open on an over-sized storage room. A stink far worse than anything before poured out on them. Tonia reeled back, gagging.

"Oh, no. Dear God, don't look, m'lady." Carlton just had time to turn from Antonia before his stomach emptied itself of the contents of his supper.

His warning came too late. She saw. The room was stacked helter-skelter, some three deep, with the decomposing bodies of children.

Tonia's stomach settled far more quickly than her head. Long after the police had taken the furious Louisa and the raving Pimm away and the coroner had begun his sad duty of clearing the room of its heartbreaking contents, her mind reeled. Sir Gerald secured a temporary warden to oversee the children in the school, but Tonia insisted on taking the small Carter children away with her. Pimm's records disclosed the location of the farm Joey had been hired out to, and Hardy was dispatched to fetch him as well. Still, even after Floss, Lettie, Sukey, and Tim— found in the dormitory hiding under a bed—were settled on pallets in the dining hall of the Magdalen House under the supervision of Nora, the new night nurse, Antonia's head reeled and her hands shook.

She was most grateful that Frederick had offered to accompany her back to Wandseley Hall in Charles's absence. "Oh, m'lady, you poor lamb!" Even before Isabella knew what had happened she took Antonia in charge. "Shock, that's what it is." She set about directing the Wandseley servants to build up the fire, bring blankets and prepare strong, hot tea.

By the time Sir Gerald returned from dealing with the authorities, equally in need of a roaring fire, tea and considerably stronger drink—a large splash of which he added to Tonia's teacup as well—she was no longer trembling and the fog that gripped her brain had begun to clear.

"I don't understand—" she began.

"It was the subsidies. When Pimm realized he lost payment for a child that died, he simply disposed of the body and left the name on the list. Most of the bodies he buried within the grounds of the school. The last winter, as you'll recall, was unusually cold. The ground froze so hard he couldn't bury those who died. So he put them in the storage room."

Tonia shook her head. "Do you have any idea how many?"

Sir Gerald took a large drink of brandy. "More than a dozen I'd say at a glance. It'll take time to sort it out. Of course, the back garden will need to be dug up."

"But—" Tonia swallowed. "The ones we found... They'll be given Christian burials?"

"Certainly. And the school cleaned and re-staffed. With more careful supervision." He shook his head. "I don't deny the corporation bear a large responsibility in this. Eight years the man was there."

"Were there no rumors?"

"Now we're hearing them. Louisa said Pimm himself reported a strange atmosphere around the school. He claimed he could hear noises—wailing, tapping and scratching. He turned to alcohol for comfort."

"His own conscience drove him mad," Tonia mused. "Still, his greed was so great he wouldn't do anything about it."

"Greed or insanity," Wandseley replied.

"What will become of him? Will he be tried?"

"I expect he'll be committed to the lunatic asylum. Of course, the police will look into it, but there doesn't seem to be any indication that Pimm hurried his orphans to their death. Unless it was by under feeding and over working them." He considered. "No, I expect the coroner will rule natural causes."

Tonia wondered what was natural in all that, but something that had been increasingly worrying her pushed forward in her mind. "What about the children?"

"We'll reorder the school."

"No, I mean the others, those of the women of the Magdalen House. And the women. Sending them back to their old life is so—so hopeless." She turned to Frederick who had returned with Sir Gerald and sat in a chair a little apart. "I've been thinking about this, Freddie. Could the refuge teach sewing? Many women take in laundry. With sewing and laundry service to offer, the Magdalen House could set up a regular laundry and employ the women once they're recovered. You might even turn a profit to fund the asylum."

"An excellent idea, Tonia. But we'd need more space. Property is unbelievably hard to get in places like Bedern."

"But why? It's in deplorable condition."

"Yes, but most of it's owned by landlords who make a great profit on the nefarious activities carried out in their ramshackle buildings. We were incredibly lucky to secure the building for the refuge when the importer who used it as a warehouse moved his operation to London. We took over his lease without having to secure permission from the owner."

"Surely he would have granted it anyway. You're such a good tenant."

"But we're not popular with our neighbors. Cleaning up the neighborhood is the last thing many want. Much more profit in drugs, prostitution and illicit liquor than in religion and rescuing abused and fallen women." He gave Tonia an ironic smile. "Don't look so shocked, sister-in-law. It's the way of the world."

Tonia suppressed a yawn and settled back against her chair. Isabella sprang forward like a mother bear protecting her young. "There now, enough of that. Can't you see my lady is fatigued?" She shook her small, dark head. "What do you think of? This is no way to treat a lady. You English. This would not happen in Spain."

Freddie and Wandseley were both on their feet. "You're quite right, Isabella." Sir Gerald sketched a bow over Tonia's hand. "I do hope you may rest well, Lady Danvers." He turned. "We should all be in our beds. Frederick, will you stay the night? You don't want to return to your priest house at this hour of the night. It's certain to be cold and comfortless."

"I would be most grateful, Sir Gerald. But I must be off sharp in the morning."

"Surely Carlotta can manage without you, Freddie," Tonia said.

"Yes, certainly. I have quite another duty to see to tomorrow. I received a note from Cecilia today. She had hoped to return in time, but as she won't be able to, she has asked me to see to it for her."

Tonia was confused. "And what is that?'

"Her prison visiting—Madge Broadbent, the prisoner she visited regularly."

"The abortionist," Tonia recalled.

"The same. The death warrant has just come down. Madge is to be executed tomorrow. Cecilia asked me to visit her. To take her what comfort I can."

"If you don't have to leave until after I've had my time with Charlie I'll accompany you, then we can go on to the asylum together." Tonia was as amazed at her words as Freddie seemed to be, but he accepted readily. "But don't breathe a word to Aunt Aelfrida. She'll think I've taken an evangelical brain fever."

And perhaps she had. All the way up the stairs Antonia wondered what she had got herself into now.

The next morning Tonia was still wondering when the Wandseley carriage deposited them in front of the Castle Prison. It was just ten years old and built in the latest style, following the example set by Pentonville, the model prison in London, with four prison blocks radiating out from the Governor's residence in front. Antonia knew that the elegance of the exterior structure would hardly be reflected in what they would face inside. Still, she was gratified that the facade was less forbidding than she had imagined.

"It's quite in the forefront of prison design," Freddie said as if he had read her mind. "The warders can observe each block from the central location. The prisoners have separate cells and receive daily religious instruction and exercise as well as their labor."

"They have useful work?" Tonia asked.

"The men are put to work quarrying, building roads and walking the treadmill to grind flour. Women and children are largely set to picking oakum."

"Oakum?"

"The loose fiber of old rope. Prisoners unravel it so it can be mixed with tar to caulk the seams in the ships of her majesty's navy."

In spite of the modern methods Freddie assured her of, Tonia took a deep breath as the warder led the way toward the condemned block. Apparently Freddie heard her for he turned with a concerned look. "You needn't do this, Tonia. You may wait in the anteroom. Or take a hackney on to the Magdalen House. I'll meet you there."

Tonia lifted her chin. Cecilia Hever was a mere slip of a girl and she did this regularly. Tonia would certainly not abandon her good intentions now. No matter how the massive stone walls seemed to close in on her. Despite her determination, however, she started when the heavy iron-studded wooden door slammed shut behind her, closing them in a cell perhaps thirteen by seven feet in size.

A small window crossed by wrought iron bars high in the wall gave the only light in the space. Tonia blinked to help her eyes adjust. The room was sparsely furnished with a stone water closet pan, a metal water-basin and a hammock slung across the cell. The mattress and blanket were folded neatly on a shelf to the left of the door.

"'S good ov ye to come." A short, stocky woman in a faded black dress and white cap rose from the three-legged stool next to the small table in the corner.

"Miss Hever was unable to come. She asked that I do so. To bring you comfort."

"Kind ov ye. An' you, too." She looked at Tonia. "Who's this?"

"I'm Antonia," she supplied before Freddie could make introductions. "I'm a friend of Cecilia's, too."

"Aye. Right thoughtful-like ov ye to bother, but don't fret none. I'll be in a better place soon."

"I know you will, Madge. We can thank the Lord that you've made real spiritual progress in your time here. I wish all prisoners would do so well." Freddie opened his Bible to read out a comforting passage.

But Madge, having made peace with her Maker and her circumstances, seemed to be more interested in a good gossip than in the Gospel. "'Ere, what o' that William Dove fellow? Dost think 'e'll get off?"

Tonia was amazed the prisoner should be so well-informed of current events.

Madge gave a gap-toothed grin. "Oh, aye, Chaplain uses 'im reg'lar as an example in 'is talks. Sold 'is soul to t' devil.

Got a right fiery sermon against that, we did. It were a fine 'un."

She smiled again. "And 'im dealin' with t' witch-man. That put the fear right up me, it did. But chaplain said I 'ad nothin' to fear if I'd repented of it."

"You consulted Harrison?" Tonia vaguely recalled Cece mentioning something about that.

Madge nodded. "Aye, I did. But not fer any ov 'is magic. It were a professional consultation, like."

"He advised you on performing abortions?"

"Not at first. Dentist 'e were. I 'ad toothache somethin' fierce. I was waitin' fer 'im to do fer my tooth, sittin' there groanin' like the end o' the world 'ad come. But even so, I 'eard 'im in t' other room, tellin' this lady 'ow to do it. I quit groanin' and listened right careful. Allus glad to learn a new trick, you know." She paused. "O' course that were in the old days. Repented I 'ave now, vicar. Before God.

"But I was 'appy enow to learn then. And when I saw what a fine lady she were I decided what's good enow fer 'er would be good enow fer my clients. No mess, you see. Just a little drink. No blood to clean up. If that silly chit I give the tincture to 'adn't taken too much and done fer 'erself I'd still be in business."

She looked quickly at Freddie, "Not that I'd want to now, vicar. Not now that I've seen the light. But that's 'ow it were."

"Who was this fine lady?" Antonia asked.

Madge gave a cackle of a laugh. "Lord love ya, we wasn't introduced."

"Did you see her?"

"Just when she left. Fine lady, like I said. Very fine. And proud. Yer can allus tell. Real tall. An' straight. Like a barge pole. Fierce red hair and bright blue dress. With ruffles, I think." Madge shrugged. "Tha's all I saw." Tonia shivered. Madge had described Carlotta Billingston to a tee.

"And Harrison advised this lady on how to prevent an abortion?"

Madge laughed so hard she had to hold her sides. "Lor', what a tonic you are. Course not. 'Ow to do it. Nice and lady-like, o' course. No apparatus. Just a few grains o' yew berry powder. No one gets 'er 'ands dirty, like."

She shook her head. "Shoulda listened more careful, though. 'Just a pinch, no more than a drachm,' 'e said. Otherwise the client dies and there it is." She spread her hands in a gesture of finality.

Tonia found it impossible to concentrate on the prayers Frederick offered for Madge Broadbent's soul, although she did manage to join in automatically for the final, "And may she rise in glory." But her mind was far too occupied with the astounding revelation that Carlotta Billingston had sought advice on how to perform an abortion from the witch-man Henry Harrison.

As soon as she and Freddie were in the cab she turned to him. "Freddie, it's Carlotta, it must be." But speaking the words showed them for the nonsense they must be. "No. That can't be right. It makes no sense. Why would she be working day and night to keep an asylum for pregnant women going?"

"Madge must have been mistaken."

"That's what I keep telling myself. But her description fit so exactly."

"There must be others who fit that description." But Freddie did not sound convinced.

Nor was Antonia. A lady of unusual height, rail thin, wearing Carlotta's favorite color and with Carlotta's red hair... It was too much to be a coincidence. And Carlotta, who kept the supply cupboard and brewed her own tonic, even had a drachm measure in her supplies.

Had she, for some incomprehensible reason, been giving

abortions to residents of the Magdalen House, perhaps in some misguided attempt to help the women, and inadvertently given an overdose that resulted in death? Or did she have a twin sister who practiced the dark arts? Tonia shook her head. She was veering into fantasy.

There was only one thing to do, she decided. She must confront Carlotta. Surely she would have an explanation.

When the Hackney rounded the corner into Andrewgate, however, all other thoughts swept from Tonia's mind at the sight of Hardy filling the aerostat at the gas main. "Stop!" She cried to the driver and jumped from the cab before Freddie could hand her down. "Hardy, is there news? Is Lord Danvers ready to return? Is he recovered?"

"Ah, m'lady," Hardy turned to her. "So there is. The post was for coming just after you left. Fine he is and waiting for me."

"Oh, wonderful news! I'll go with you, Hardy. Just wait here. I must check on Millie. I'll be right back."

Tonia rounded the corner to the asylum in such a rush that she almost walked straight into a small man with a sweeping mustache wearing a check waistcoat on the doorstep. Her brain registered that she had met him, but she couldn't place where. He apparently had no such problem, however, because he pulled his bowler hat from his head and made her a sweeping bow. "Lady Danvers, a pleasure to see you again."

Now she remembered. "Mr. Billingston. Forgive me. I'm afraid I'm in rather a rush."

He bowed again and stepped into a waiting carriage, which Tonia recognized as the one she had often seen Lady Billingston arrive in.

Tonia yanked the door of the Magdalen House open, but just inside the refuge she stopped at the sound of raised voices coming from Carlotta's office. "You're hysterical, girl. Do as I say." Lady Billingston's voice rose with authority.

The garbled words and cry that followed were Millie's. Was she in labour? Antonia hurried forward, leaving the door open behind herself.

"It were 'im. 'E's the one wot took me. It's 'is child."

"Nonsense. How would a prostitute know? Now drink this."

Millie screamed and ran from the room, all but cannoning into Tonia.

Tonia could make little sense of it all, but it was clear Millie was desperate. Antonia grabbed the girl's hand and pulled her out the door. Hardy should still be around the corner with the balloon. He could help them. She was vaguely aware of Carlotta following them as she led Millie around the corner. There was Hardy with the aerostat and Freddie assisting him.

Tonia pushed Millie forward. "Go on, they'll help you." She looked back and saw that Carlotta had now been joined by her husband who was charging like a mad bull. "Freddie!" Tonia shouted.

Freddie lifted Millie from the pavement and set her in the gondola beside Hardy who was securing the ballast bags. "Get down," he ordered.

But Millie didn't hide. Instead she stood and pointed. "'E's the one! Ah saw 'im. Ah—Ow!" She doubled over with a cry of pain.

Tonia clambered into the gondola to help her.

Freddie turned to face the pursuers. "Sylvester, what is—" he began, then stopped when Sylvester Billingston pulled a knife from his pocket.

"I'll cut her tongue out, the silly, lying—" he lunged toward Millie, but Freddie was quicker. He stuck his foot out and Sylvester catapulted toward the gondola, knife extended.

It wasn't until the aerostat had reached the level of the rooftops that anyone realized that in his plunge Sylvester had sliced the tether rope.

Tonia looked over the side of the gondola to see the incongruous sight of a cassock-clad vicar shouting for a policeman while he held a squirming man in one arm and a raging woman in the other. The arm lock he was applying had undoubtedly been learned in the Oxford boxing society.

But Tonia's amusement was short-lived as she turned at a sharp cry from Millie. "What is it? Are you hurt?"

"It's the babe. It's comin'!"

"Oh, my goodness. Hardy, can you set us down?"

"Not in the city, m'lady. No room."

"Well, then, find a field somewhere."

"Ow!" Another cry from Millie told her the pains were coming fast. And hard. What did she recall of her own confinement that would be of use here? The aerostat certainly offered no room for Millie to lie down.

"Kneel! Get on your knees, Millie. Hold on to the edge of the Gondola when you need to push." Tonia knelt beside her and reached under the girls' thin skirt to remove her undergarments. There was no time to be delicate in these matters. Besides, Hardy was far too busy guiding the aerostat.

Millie was sobbing now. "Breathe, Millie. Short, shallow pants. Like a dog. Don't hold your breath." A gush of warm fluid soaked both their skirts. "Don't worry, Millie. That's good. It won't be long now."

Tonia wished she could see, but the best she could do was feel the warm, moist region between the girl's legs. Her fingers touched something round and slick. "I feel the head!" Tonia was amazed at the surge of excitement that flooded through her.

"You're doing fine, Millie. Can you spread your legs any

wider? Good. That's good. Now when the next pain comes, push. Hard."

Millie's cry was enough to frighten the birds from the trees. And it was matched by Tonia's exultant shout as a tiny, red bundle of new life slipped into her waiting hands. "Oh, oh, oh!" Was all she could say, over and over again. "It's a girl," she almost sobbed. "And she's beautiful."

Then she realized there were things she needed to do. What had the midwife done when Charlie was born? Tonia had been lulled by her whiff of chloroform, but she remembered being ecstatic—and exhausted. She couldn't remember much else. She did recall, though, the joy of hearing her babe's first tiny squall of a cry.

The infant in her arms was not crying. "Oh, come now—cry!" Rather as a reflex she held the baby up and a waft of cool air rushed over her. With that, the infant screwed up her tiny face, opened her mouth and let out a wail.

Tonia relaxed. One thing she did remember from her own experience—she would never forget—the midwife had almost instantly opened Tonia's gown and put her tiny, miraculous baby to her breast. 'The wee'un needs to suckle, m'lady. It'll help your insides come right,' the midwife had said. And then the wonderful feeling of the tiny mouth groping and, after some prodding from the midwife, closing over her nipple. Tonia felt a warmth at her own breast with the memory.

"Here, lean back," she directed Millie. "Open your dress." It took several minutes of fumbling in the crowded space but they achieved it to the accompaniment of Millie's coos and squeaks and tiny snorts from the babe. Tonia wrapped Millie's discarded petticoat around mother and babe for warmth.

Then Tonia recalled another, less comfortable task the midwife had performed. "Millie, I need to push on your abdomen. It might hurt a bit, but there's more that needs to come out."

"More! Ah'm not 'avin' twins?"

Tonia laughed. "No, don't worry. Afterbirth it's called. The sacque the baby was in—it needs to come out. Millie grunted with discomfort when Tonia pushed, and Tonia found it awkward working around the still-attached umbilical cord, but in the end all came right. At last Tonia looked up where Hardy was studiously keeping his eyes on the valves and upper ropes of the aerostat. "It's all right, Hardy. You can look now."

He bent over to observe his newest passenger just as a large white bird flew by. "Well as I live and breathe, my old granny was always telling it was the stork that brought bairns, but I never believed her until now.

"What will you be calling her?"

Millie looked at Antonia shyly and bit her lip. "Well, Ah was thinkin', if it wouldn't be too great a liberty," she paused. "Ah'd be reet 'appy to call 'er Antonia."

"I would be honoured. And I'll be happy to stand godmother for her if you'd like."

Millie looked blank.

"Oh, my dear, you don't mean to say you haven't been baptized?" She laughed. "Well, that will be a task for Freddie. Won't he be delighted to make Christians of you all!"

Still sitting on the floor of the gondola next to Millie, Tonia heaved a great sigh of contentment. "Do you have any idea where we are, Hardy? Can you set us down very gently?"

22

A few minutes later when Hardy performed the softest landing of his aeronautical career, Tonia looked out across the landing field and gave a cry. "Hardy, you're a genius! How did you manage to bring us back to Wandseley Hall?"

"It was seeming the best plan, m'lady. And we had a fair breeze."

Tonia's cry of delight was even greater when she saw the tall, darkly handsome man in a black top hat striding across the field toward them. "Charles!" She scrambled over the edge of the gondola and threw herself into his arms. "How is this possible? I thought you were at Harrogate!"

"Since it seems my man had better things to do than to collect me I accompanied the charming Misses Hever on the train."

"Oh, Charles, you won't believe it! So much has happened! I can't wait to tell you—"

To her surprise, Charles thrust her from him with a horrified look on his face. "Antonia, what in the world—you're covered with blood."

"Oh, yes! And just wait until you see the inside of your gondola. It was absolutely wonderful!"

"Tonia, you're raving." And he took the most immediate means at hand to quieten her, simply placing his lips over hers in a long, deep kiss.

Considerably later, after an equally appalled Isabella had refreshed Antonia's toilette and Nurse Bevans had done everything necessary for Tonia's tiny new namesake and her mother, they were all gathered in the front bedroom where Lady Wandseley had installed Millie to try to make sense of all that had happened.

Tonia, sitting next to her husband and holding The Honourable Charles Frederick on her lap, smiled as she heard Danvers humming soft strains of *Soa Gân* to their son. Antonia turned toward the pale but smiling figure propped against pillows in the high tester bed. "So Millie, are you saying that Sylvester Billingston is, er—" she sought a delicate way to phrase her question.

But Millie was more accustomed to being direct in such matters. "'E's the father, an' that's the truth." She blushed and looked down. "Ah couldn't pay t' rent, you see."

"Billingston was your landlord?" Danvers sounded as shocked as Tonia felt.

"That's quite true," Freddie, recently arrived to tell them about the successful conclusion of his morning with the arrival of Sergeant Carlton and the incongruous sight of the proud Carlotta Billingston being taken off in a police van, spoke up. "I'd had no time to tell you, but after Antonia put forward the idea of opening a sewing school and laundry next to the Magdalen House I checked the public records with the idea of trying to secure more space. I discovered that Sylvester Billingston owns most of Bedern."

Tonia shook her head. "Carlotta Billingston, married to a slum landlord and a——" once again she couldn't find a polite word to finish her sentence.

"I believe libertine is the term you're looking for, my dear." Charles spoke quietly in her ear, but even so, they received a sharp look from the Dowager Duchess seated across from them.

"But why would Lady Billingston want to poison all those mothers and their children? They couldn't all have been..."

"Sylvester's offspring?" Again Charles finished Tonia's sentence. "No, but I rather suspect Polly's might have been. That would account for the rather special treatment she received."

"But Polly wasn't on the street. She was a respectable girl."

Philomena Wandseley paused in her act of pouring cups of tea, which her husband was handing around. "Oh, my, I never thought." She paused and bit her lip. "I wonder—I had a simply abysmal case of grippe early last May and I sent Polly to take my place at the asylum a few times. I didn't want to let them down as I knew how shorthanded they were.

"It was only two or three times because one night Polly returned dreadfully late and terribly upset. Then she came down with a mild case of grippe herself..." Philomena put her hand to her throat. "Oh, how dreadful!"

"The day Polly died, had she been anywhere near the Magdalen House?" Tonia asked.

Lady Wandseley considered. "Yes, she had. I sent her to collect a book I had left there. I thought I would want to read it that night."

"And she took the chance to ask Carlotta, whom she knew worked with herbs, if she could help her." Tonia considered for a moment. "It's unlikely, though that Carlotta would have had the laurel water at the refuge. She must have procured it from her cook and brought it with her to the dinner party that night." Tonia considered for a moment. "Carlotta might have suspected who the father was. Perhaps her husband had come by to collect her when Polly was there and she wasn't ready to leave yet..."

Danvers took her hand. "Speculation my love."

"Yes, but it makes sense. And it explains why Polly was given quite a different tincture from the others. Carlotta wouldn't have wanted anything to link Polly's condition to the asylum."

"Yes," Danvers said. "I've been trying to work that out. I'm certain the bottle that killed Polly contained laurel extract—"

"But none of the bottles at the asylum smelled like almond," Tonia finished.

Heads turned toward a sharp clearing of the throat from a newcomer just inside the doorway. "Hardy," Danvers greeted his man.

"Yes, m'lord, I don't like to be interrupting. I just came to say your gondola cleaned up fine, so as you wouldn't be worrying, but I did hear, and you need to be knowing that I had those bottles analyzed like Lady Antonia asked."

Tonia had completely forgotten. "Oh, good, Hardy. What did you learn?"

"Two of 'em was just what they ought to be—*laurus nobilis*. It was the third one. Enough yew extract to be for killing a horse." He paused. "Er—so to speak that is."

"Thank you, Hardy, that's most helpful. Be sure you pass those bottles on to Sergeant Carlton with your report."

Tonia paused and frowned. "But I still don't understand. These women weren't likely to say anything. And who would have believed them—or cared who the father was? Why bother poisoning the women her husband..." It seemed Tonia kept getting herself into dead ends. "And that doesn't explain the others," she finished.

"I think it was quite another motive," Danvers said. "And it explains her 'devotion' to the refuge. Freddie, you said you obtained the lease to the property from the former occupant without going through the landlord and that many of your neighbors weren't any too happy at your attempts to make the area respectable."

"That's absolutely right. There's far more profit in vice than in virtue," Frederick agreed.

"I believe Carlotta Billingston was working day and night to discredit the Magdalen House. When word spread that women were dying there unnaturally soon no one would come and you would have to close down. Then Billingston could rent it out as a house of prostitution or the like."

"Do you think she gave Victoria poisoned tonic, too?" Tonia asked.

"Most certainly, I should think," Danvers said. "The death of a volunteer would have guaranteed doom for the refuge. Respectable women would have assumed she contracted some sickness from the work there and refused to volunteer themselves."

The room was quiet for a moment as everyone worked through the tangled puzzle. "I do believe you've solved it." Freddie was the first to speak. "And Carlotta might very well have been successful if you hadn't acceded to my plea for help. I never realized how useful it could be to have an amateur sleuth in the family.

"Funny thing about that, though. When I was holding Billingston waiting for the police he was ranting, calling you and Antonia every name in the book—well, mostly names that aren't in books—and he said he thought he'd fixed you and it was a pity he'd failed. What do you think he meant by that?"

Tonia's brow furrowed. "I can't imagine..." Then she gasped. "The fire! Norwood! Could Billingston possibly have been responsible for that? I thought it was my carelessness with leaving a candle burning. Oh, my goodness..." She leaned back against the sofa, her head spinning. Could it be?

"Yes!" She sat up again with a jolt. "Now I recall. That first night—I was trying to make conversation with Sylvester Billingston—and hard going it was. I asked him if he knew Northamptonshire. He said he didn't, but he let slip that his wife's family was from there."

Danvers nodded slowly. "Hmm, yes, it's just possible. He could have bribed a servant among his connections to set the fire. But how would he have known we were even thinking of coming to York? We weren't, until after the fire."

"Afraid that's my fault," Freddie spoke up. "After the third death occurred I told Carlotta not to worry—that I would write straight away to my brother who was famous for his detective skills and he would get to the bottom of it if there was anything unnatural going on."

"How ironic. If not for the fire I would never have been able to talk Charles into coming to York, would I, my love?"

"Indeed not, but I'm most glad you did."

"It's what I always say." The Dowager Duchess set her teacup aside. "The devil always overplays his hand."

"Aunt Aelfrida, surely you don't mean to say that the devil made me do it?" Danvers grinned at her.

"Don't be impertinent, young man. I'm quite certain the authorities will sort out all of that. I'm concerned about matters much closer to home. Philomena," She turned to Lady Wandseley. "You must take Millie on." She indicated the new mother dozing against her pillows with a contented look on her face. "Can't send the gel back to the slums after all this, and you need a replacement for Polly." Lady Wandseley blanched, but she didn't argue.

"As for the children," She turned to Sir Gerald. "As soon as you and that incompetent corporation of yours sort out the school it will be quite adequate. I can't imagine how you let it get into such a state, but I expect you've learned your lesson." Sir Gerald looked appropriately penitent.

"As for the others, Frederick has told me of the plan to expand the work of The Magdalen House. Since no one else here seems to be capable of undertaking such a work satisfactorily I shall become patroness. And I shall see to it that all my friends subscribe as well." She nodded at the amazed silence her announcement produced. "There now. That will do very well."

Freddie was the first to react. He sprang to his feet, crossed the room, and planted a kiss on the papery cheek of the Dowager Duchess of Aethelbert. "Aunt Aelfrida, you are a sport."

"That is quite enough young man. I shall have to take you in hand, too."

"Yes, please do, your grace. I shall certainly need all the help I can get." A smiling Victoria stood in the doorway, radiant in a pastel flounced gown with pink flowers in her blond curls.

Freddie all but ran to pull her forward into the room with Cecilia right behind her. Freddie put his arm around Victoria's tiny waist and opened his mouth to speak, but no words came out.

"It seems that my nephew is, for once, at a loss for words." The Dowager Duchess's words were crisp, but her smile looked exceedingly pleased. "As usual, it falls to me to do everything. I must tell you that my nephew has come to his senses and has realized he is not called to celibacy."

Antonia could only assume Freddie did the right thing and kissed his fiancé. For her part, she was much too thoroughly engaged in a similar activity with Frederick's elder brother.

HISTORICAL FOOTNOTES

Dove's case was appealed to the Home Secretary and great support for leniency was filed, especially by the Wesleyan Methodists. In spite of the vigorous efforts made to procure a mitigation of the sentence, however, including several petitions sent to Queen Victoria herself at Buckingham Palace, Dove was executed at York on Saturday, August 9, 1856.

The day before, Dove freely admitted to his Methodist prison visitor Mr. Wright that he had poisoned his wife and that for the offense he ought to die. Before ascending the steps to the scaffold he said, "Tell my poor mother I die happy."

Owen Davies, author of the book *Murder, Magic, Madness*, has examined William Dove's case in the terms of modern psychology and suggests that his behavior was typical of bipolar disorder or manic depression which was not recognized until the end of the nineteenth century.

Although the account of George Pimm and the York Industrial Ragged School sounds like something dreamed up by a darker version of Charles Dickens, I must assure you it is quite historical. Pimm was declared mad and taken to the lunatic asylum, where he stayed for the rest of his life, which wasn't long. After four months of incarceration, he hung himself. In a suicide note he complained of the wailings and screams of the dead children that tortured him in his cell.

Visitors to the Bedern area have spoken of feeling their clothing or bags being tugged as they walked through the Bedern Arch. Some people have heard children's laughter.

As to my other villains, purely fictional though they were, I am certain they were far too calculating for their counsel to attempt to enter a plea of insanity on their behalf.

MAJOR REFERENCES

Davies, Owen, *Murder, Magic, Madness*: The Victorian Trials of Dove and the Wizard, 2005, Pearson Education Ltd. UK

Williams, Caleb, M.D., *Observations on the Criminal Responsibility of the Insane*; founded on the trials of James Bill and of William Dove, 1856, John Churchill, London.

Browne, G. Lathom and Stewart, C. G., *Murder by Poisoning*; by Prussic Acid, Strychnia, Antimony, Arsenic and Aconitia, 1883, Stevens and Sons, London.

ABOUT THE AUTHOR

Donna Fletcher Crow has always loved the Victorians. "I love their energy, their confidence, their optimism. Victorians are often criticized as being repressed and are blamed for the injustices in their society; but I see them as people who sincerely worked for good. There were many difficulties in Victorian society, but when they identified a problem they set about with enormous vigor to correct it. I hope I have portrayed those achievements in some of the novels I have set in that period."

Crow is a lifelong Anglophile, a former English teacher, and the author of 50 books, mostly novels of British history, including the award-winning Arthurian epic *Glastonbury*, The Novel of Christian England. She currently authors three mystery series. You can see more about her books and pictures from her research trips at www.DonnaFletcherCrow.com.

Subscribe to her newsletter here:
www.donnafletchercrow.com/subscribe.php

BOOKS BY DONNA FLETCHER CROW

The Elizabeth & Richard Literary Suspense Mysteries:

The Shadow of Reality

Elizabeth and Richard at a Dorothy L Sayers mystery week high in the Rocky Mountains

A Midsummer Eve's Nightmare

Elizabeth and Richard honeymoon at a Shakespeare Festival in Ashland, Oregon

A Jane Austen Encounter

A second honeymoon visit to Jane Austen's homes turns deadly

The Torch Ignites

Elizabeth and Richard look back to their first meeting in a New England autumn

A Most Singular Venture

Murder in Jane Austen's London

The Monastery Murders, Clerical Mysteries

A Very Private Grave

Legendary buried treasure, a brutal murder and lurking danger—

an itinerary of terror across a holy terrain

A Darkly Hidden Truth

Ancient puzzles, modern murder and breathless chase scenes

through a remote, waterlogged landscape

An Unholy Communion

An idyllic pilgrimage through Wales

becomes a deadly struggle between good and evil

A Newly Crimsoned Reliquary

Murder stalks the shadows of Oxford's hallowed shrines

An All-Consuming Fire

A Christmas wedding in a monastery—

if the bride can defeat the murderer prowling the Yorkshire moors

The Lord Danvers Investigates,
Victorian True-Crime Mysteries

A Most Inconvenient Death

The brutal Stanfield Hall murders shatter a quiet Norwich community and pull Danvers from deep personal grief into a dangerous investigation.

Grave Matters

Lord and Lady Danvers's honeymoon in Scotland is interrupted by the ghosts of Burke and Hare-style grave robbers.

To Dust You Shall Return

Catherine Bacon is murdered in the very shadow of Canterbury Cathedral but Charles and Antonia are overwhelmed with their own problems.

A Tincture of Murder

William Dove is on trial in York for poisoning his wife while Lord and Lady Danvers struggle to assist in a refuge home where fallen women continue to die mysteriously.

Where There is Love Historical Romance

Where Love Begins

Where Love Illumines

Where Love Triumphs

Where Love Restores

Where Love Shines

Where Love Calls

Printed in Great Britain
by Amazon

80341794R00129